In the Heart of a Mustang

In the Heart of a Mustang

M.J. Evans

M.J. Evans/ Dancing Horse Press
7013 S. Telluride St.
Foxfield, CO 80016

www.dancinghorsepress.com

Publisher's Note: This is a work of fiction. Names, characters, places, and incidents are a product of the author's imagination. Locales and public names are sometimes used for atmospheric purposes. Any resemblance to actual people, living or dead, or to businesses, companies, events, institutions, or locales is completely coincidental.

Ordering Information: Special discounts are available on quantity purchases by corporations, associations, and others. For details, contact the publisher at the address above.

First Edition

ISBN-13: 978-1-946229-67-0

Printed in the United States of America

Distributed by Bublish, Inc.
Bublish.com

Everyone needs loyalty, love, and at times

healing.

Lucky is the soul who finds all three

In the Heart of a Mustang.

CHAPTER 1

AT-After Truth

IT WAS IN THE FALL of his sophomore year that Hunter learned the truth and that changed everything.

A feeling of crispness tinged the air, typical of autumn. The sun shone brightly from its lowered southern position, and discarded leaves bounced around the sidewalks and streets.

The fifteen-year-old boy clutched his violin case in one hand and his essay in the other as he ran from the bus stop toward the large complex of luxury apartments where he and his mom lived. He was excited to share the teacher's comments with her. He had been struggling with school the last couple of years.

He just couldn't seem to get motivated enough to perform at the level to which both he and his mother knew he was capable. The one thing at which he truly excelled was the violin. But he had done well on this paper and he knew his mom would be pleased with the "B" that was written boldly on the top.

He swung open the door of the high rise and dashed into the foyer. Before he even reached the staircase, he heard the shouting. He recognized his mother's voice immediately. The other voice was unfamiliar. It was a male voice, loud and harsh. He bounded up the stairs two and three at a time, turned the corner and came to an abrupt stop in front of apartment 201, their home for the last year.

"I want you to leave right now! Hunter will be home any minute, and I don't want him to see you," the boy heard his mother say.

"Why not, my love. Are you ashamed of me?" responded the stranger.

"I am not your love! Now get out! Get away from here and never bother us again!"

"I just want to see my son. Surely you won't deny me that much?"

The door swung open and his mother, with her back to him, facing the stranger, pointed back toward the door. "I said leave. Now!" she shouted at the man.

The stranger was now in full view through the open doorway. Hunter caught his breath. He felt as though he were looking in a mirror. He had the bizarre impression that he was viewing a much older and harder version of himself. The strange man's features were just like his. The blue eyes, the long straight nose, even the dirty, shaggy hair was the same sandy blond color of his own. Suddenly the mirror seemed to shatter and sharp shards of glass pierced his heart. Hunter could feel himself caving inward from the pain. This man...this man...this was his *father*. He knew it instantly. His heart told him so, even as it seemed to split apart at the seams.

But how could that be? His father was dead, killed in the war while saving the lives of countless others. His father was a hero, the kind of man he was supposed to become...or so he had always been told.

Hunter froze in place. He wanted to turn and run, but he couldn't get his body to respond. He felt as though someone had snuck in and nailed his feet to the floor.

As Hunter stared at this stranger, a wry smile formed across the man's face. But it was not the kind of loving smile a father gives his son, the kind he always imagined his father would give him if he saw him in person. It was not even a warm, welcoming, nice-to-meet-you type of smile. His mouth was formed into what could better be described as a sneer. The boy's mother turned around. Seeing Hunter, she gasped and her hand flew to her mouth. Immediately, she stepped up to Hunter and put her arms around him, placing her body between the boy and the man.

"So, here he is. The spitin' image of his old man. A real chip off the old block."

Melody whirled around. "No. He isn't anything like you. He's good and kind."

"*Good and kind,*" the man mocked. "Well ain't that sweet. Give me a little time with him and we'll see what we can do about that!"

"I said leave. Now!" snapped Melody.

"Not when I'm just getting acquainted with my son!"

Melody left Hunter's side and dashed back into their apartment, returning a few seconds later with the small handgun she kept in the drawer beside her bed. She raised her arms, clasping the gun in both hands. Her hands were steady but her voice trembled slightly. "You leave now. I know how to use this and I'm not afraid to. In fact, it would be a pleasure."

The man's eyes widened in surprise. He turned back to Hunter. "Well, I guess I'll just be goin' now, *son*," said the man as he stepped through the doorway. "I can see I ain't wanted here," he added as he brushed by him, trailing a strong scent of fresh liquor and stale tobacco.

Once through the doorway, the man stopped and looked back. "You'll regret you treated me this way, Melody. Mark my works, you'll regret it!" He turned and stomped down the stairs, a deep and almost cruel laughter floating up the stairs behind him. The loud, retreating footsteps vibrated in Hunter's head. The laughter stung his ears and suffocated his heart.

Hunter's mother took a step back and looked at her son, love and concern mixing together on her face. She set the gun on a shelf by the door, slid her hands down his arms and took his hands in hers. "Come in the house, sweetheart," she said as she gently pulled him toward the doorway.

Still, Hunter could not get himself to move. He felt as though he had been turned to stone. He couldn't, wouldn't, look at her. Instead, his mind focused on the long, black tunnel in front of him. There was no light around him or ahead of him.

A painful memory burst to the surface after years of being buried where no one would find it. In the vision that appeared in the darkness, Hunter was ten. He was visiting his grandparents on their farm in Grand Junction, Colorado.

On one particularly hot and dry western Colorado day, when the air was heavy and the sun vicious, Hunter and his cousin, Ethan, decided to find relief by going fishing in the Colorado River. The brown water of the river flowed lazily past the northern border of the farm. With fishing poles in one hand and a bucket of worms from Grandma's garden in the other, the boys alternately skipped and strolled across the horse pasture. The two old, long-ago retired horses lifted their heads from their seemingly perpetual grazing just long enough to examine their visitors. Their curiosity was quickly satisfied and they dropped their heads in unison and returned to their eating.

The boys shimmied under the bottom wire of the fence and settled their gear on the shore. Once worms were securely threaded on the hooks, they cast their lines into the backwater of an eddy.

"Guess what?" said Ethan.

"What?"

"You promise you won't tell anyone?"

"Sure," responded Hunter, always happy to be brought into his older cousin's confidences.

"My dad is getting a new job and we are moving far away."

Hunter looked at the older boy in surprise. "Where are you moving to?"

"Clear across the country to Atlanta. That's a city in Georgia."

"Wow, that's cool. But why can't I tell anyone?"

"Dad wants to tell Grandma and Grandpa himself. He's afraid they might be sad to have us move so far away."

Hunter nodded. This made perfect sense. Grandma and Grandpa loved having their family close by.

"My dad is getting a big promotion in his company," Ethan continued. "He's super smart and his bosses think he is the best at what he does. I'm not really sure what that is but it's pretty important."

Hunter looked over at Ethan. "My dad was super smart, too. If he was still alive, he'd probably be a bigwig in a big company too."

Ethan scoffed. "Your dad? Your dad is nothing but a thief and a drug dealer. What do you mean *if* he was alive? He *is* alive and rotting away in some jail cell somewhere! Your father is a bad man. He's nothing more than a bum!"

Hunter dropped his rod and dove for Ethan, knocking him down on his back. With both fists, he punched at his cousin's face and pulled at his hair while Ethan struggled to get him off his chest and control the flailing fists.

"Get off me! What do you think you're doing? Ouch! Geez! You're a madman," exclaimed Ethan as he rolled away and managed to maneuver his body a safe distance from his young cousin.

Hunter remained kneeling on the sand, his hands hurting and hanging to his sides. He dropped his head and let the tears flow freely down his cheeks. He sniffed and rubbed his nose. "Why would you lie about my dad like that?"

Ethan got to his feet and brushed off his clothes. His fingers carefully examined the bruises he could feel gathering like storm clouds on his face. "I wasn't lying. It's true...every bit of it!"

Hunter's anger exploded within him once again, and it took all his self-control to keep from diving at his cousin a second time. "It is not! My dad was a war hero. He saved hundreds, probably *thousands* of men. And I am going to grow up to be just like him," he spat out.

"Well, I sure hope not!" was the retort as Ethan picked up his fishing pole and shimmied back under the fence.

Hunter watched him go. His heart was pounding loudly. His breathing was shallow and came in quick spurts. Sweat beaded up on his forehead and ran down the center of his back. His hands curled into tight fists, pulling at the cut skin on his knuckles. For the first time in his life, he knew the feeling of hate.

The painful images vanished instantly when Hunter heard his mother's voice. It seemed to echo from somewhere in the darkness. It was impossible to make sense of the sounds. Gradually, he became aware that his body was being pulled in some direction and eventually felt it folded over and pressed down. He felt his fingers, which were still clutched tightly around the handle of the violin case, being pried open. He blinked his eyes several times and shook his head, trying to make sense of his surroundings.

"Can I bring you a glass of milk?" he heard his mother say.

Slowly, he turned his head toward the sound of his mother's voice and looked into her pleading eyes. He swallowed hard. His voice came out as a whisper. "You lied to me."

His mother dropped her head and the tears began to flow. She slumped down beside him on the couch and took his stiff, cold hand. "I. Am. So. Sorry."

He turned sharply toward her. "You lied to me," he repeated, this time with more force and volume.

Still crying but now harder, she whispered, "I only wanted to protect you."

For the first time, his mother's tears had no effect on him. "How can lying protect me?

And just what were you trying to protect me from? From *him*?" he nearly spat out the last word.

"Yes. I didn't want you to know what kind of man your father really is. I wanted you to be proud of the father you never had. I wanted you to look up to someone."

"I look up to Grandpa. I look up to Uncle Jack. Why wasn't that enough? Why did you have to make up someone who doesn't exist?"

Melody sobbed. "I just wanted you to have a father you could be proud of."

"Then why did you pick *him* to be my father?" he said with a sneer.

"Oh, Hunter, he wasn't always like that," she said, wiping at the tears that streamed down her cheeks. "When I first met him, your father was wonderful...like the man I described to you. He was kind, smart..."

Hunter rolled his eyes and snorted.

His mother ignored it and continued. "At least that's how I viewed him." She paused. "You know, Hunter, sometimes people can start out one way but when life gets through with them...well...sometimes life changes people." She let out a long sigh. "Sometimes life changes people," she repeated softly.

The emotional trauma Hunter was going through caused him to retreat to his bed early. He instantly fell asleep, but sleep only lasted for two or three hours before he ran from his dreams and awoke, jerking up in his bed, his heart pounding, his breathing short and shallow. His mind replayed the previous day's scene over and over as though on a loop. He tried desperately to erase the image from his mind's eye as one would chalk from a blackboard. But nothing seemed to work. He tossed and turned, his sweating body dampening his sheets.

Hunter was experiencing one of those watershed moments, like the great Continental Divide, that splits a life into a before and an after. Years later, as he looked back, he would measure his life from this point: BT, Before the Truth, and AT, After the Truth. He would spend many hours pondering how life might have been if it had never happened, if he had just remained in BT.

AT meant that life for Hunter and Melody changed from that day onward. Hunter never did show his mother the essay. He found it a few days later on the floor of his room, sitting next to his open violin case.   He bent down and slammed the case shut, snapping the latches closed. He callously pushed the black case under the bed with his foot. Scooping up the essay, the boy wadded it into a ball and tossed it in his over-flowing garbage can.

CHAPTER 2

Metamorphosis

THE SCHOOL BUS DISGORGED its cargo of loud, boisterous, young teens, just as it did every morning. Hunter stepped onto the curb, stopped and stared at the door of the school. The girl behind him bumped into his backpack.

"Hey, watch where you're goin'!" he snarled.

With a look of genuine shock on her face, the girl meekly responded, "Sorry, Hunter. I didn't mean to bump you." She scurried around him and headed into the school.

Hunter felt a moment of guilt at the way he had spoken to her, but only a moment. That was the old Hunter. The BT Hunter. He pursed his lips, dropped his chin and looked up through his eyelashes and knotted brows. Instead of walking into the school, he turned left and walked down the sidewalk, across the street and away from his old life.

A few blocks later, he reached the business district of the suburban city. He was shocked to see that there were people, and even kids, out and about. He had somehow always assumed that people either went to work or went to school every day. The fact that some people just spent their days hanging out was something that had never occurred to him before.

The suffering teen found his way to a small city park and sat down under a tree, resting his back against the large, solid trunk, thinking how good it felt to let something support him. Hunter stared blankly ahead as he unconsciously picked at the dry leaves that littered the ground. He crushed them in the palms of his hands.

Memories of meeting his father continued to play and replay through his mind. He could see his father's cold, cruel eyes, his father's mouth curled into a sneer, the thin yet muscular body looming over him.

Images.

Brutal images.

They seemed to have a life of their own and never die.

Suddenly, he could sit no longer. He had to escape the pain.

He leapt to his feet and began running. The young teen's feet pounded the sidewalk ferociously. He ran until his legs and lungs hurt. Still, he kept going, hoping the pain would overshadow the aching in his heart. It didn't. He pumped his arms and continued on. At last, his body gave out and he collapsed on a bench that had been mercifully placed in front of a city bus stop. He fell forward, resting his forearms on his thighs, his hands desperately clutching one another. A guttural moan arose from deep within him, and he let himself cry. His shoulders shook as he sobbed loudly.

Hunter had rarely cried before. Not really. Oh sure, he'd had the little-kid-fall-off-a-bike-and-skin-your-knee type of cry. But this wasn't like that. This was real. This left his chest throbbing, his throat aching and his face and eyes sore and puffy.

He remembered, as a small boy, finding his mom crying for what seemed no reason. She always hugged him and told him that crying was good. It made you feel better. It was a pain drain.

But she'd been wrong. It didn't make Hunter feel better. It wasn't a pain drain at all. The pain was still there, pounding and kicking and clawing at his insides. Yes, she had been wrong. Or maybe that was just another one of her lies.

Suddenly Hunter was aware of the presence of someone else on the bench. He turned his head and jerked back as he looked into the eyes of a young man, probably ten years his senior.

"Havin' a rough go of it today?" the young man asked kindly.

Hunter turned away and didn't answer.

"It's okay, you don't have to answer. It's none of my business really. I've just had days like that myself."

Hunter stole a sideways glance at his uninvited companion. The boy noticed that the man was handsome and well groomed, but more than that, this stranger possessed a certain charisma that called out "follow me."

Hunter and the man sat silently, side-by-side. The boy looked around him and realized he had no idea where he was. He didn't recognize this part of town. The streets were car and litter-lined. The stores looked old, ill maintained and sported black bars over the windows. Many of the businesses were pawnshops, liquor stores, or tattoo parlors. A chain-link fence blocked the entrance to a weed-filled vacant lot directly across the street from where he sat. The wires had served to catch leaves, papers and plastic bags and support tall, gangly morning glory vines, wilting now with the arrival of fall.

"Where am I?" Hunter asked the man quietly, without looking at him.

"You're on the corner of Federal and Twenty-eighth. Where are you trying to go?"

Hunter shook his head. "Nowhere in particular."

"Just away?"

Hunter turned and looked at the man. His mouth turned up in a crooked smile. "I guess you could say that."

The man nodded with empathy. "Yeah, I've been on the same journey myself."

"Yeah, well, I guess I'd better get back home."

"Where do you live?"

"Off Smithville Road."

The man let out a long whistle. "That's a long way from here, boy." He reached into his pants pocket and pulled out several quarters. "Here's bus fare, enough for today and tomorrow if you want to come back and talk. I'll be here at eleven in the morning."

Exhausted and sick at heart, Melody sat in her cherry-wood rocker, intently watching the clock on the living room wall as her bare feet pushed the rocker rapidly back and forth. The young mother shifted her position and crossed and uncrossed her arms and legs.

Several hours earlier, Melody had left work the minute the school called to say Hunter was not in class. She hoped to find him at home feeling ill. Instead, she found the apartment empty. Her heart sank as her pulse quickened. Her stomach quivered as a wave of nausea swept over her.

For the next four hours, she paced back and forth across the living room, checking the clock with each turn, sitting in her rocker and rapidly pumping forward and back, then standing and pacing again. At one point, she even called the school back to see if he had turned up there.

Once school was out, calls to Mrs. Wells, his violin teacher, and friends from school had turned up nothing...no one had seen or heard from him.

By the time Hunter appeared in the entry hall, she had worked herself into a near frenzy. Gasping for breath to calm herself, she looked at her son, feeling a potent mix of anger and relief. She controlled herself enough to simply say, "We'll talk after dinner."

Dinner was eaten in silence.

With the table cleared and the dishes cleaned up, Melody called her son into the living room. She patted the couch, inviting him to sit down beside her.

Hunter remained standing, his arms tightly crossed over his chest.

The young mother, unaccustomed to having to deal with this type of behavior, took a deep breath. She tried to calm her beating heart. Wiping the nervous perspiration off her forehead, she decided to get right to the point. "The school called me at work today to tell me that you weren't in your classes."

"Yeah, so?"

The question didn't deserve a response. After another deep breath, she started again. "I know you are angry with me and want to punish me somehow. I can't say I blame you one bit. In fact, I would probably feel the same way." Hunter rolled his eyes. His stiff body, set jaw and crossed arms communicated complete boredom and disinterest and a healthy measure of disgust.

Melody ignored his response and kept going with the speech she had rehearsed in her mind all during dinner. "This behavior is only going to hurt you. It will only destroy the life you can create for yourself. Don't throw away everything you have going for you," she said with a mixture of sorrow and pleading in her eyes.

Hunter looked away. The boy didn't like that he felt sorry for her. She had spent a lifetime lying to him. She deserved any pain she felt. Yes, she deserved whatever pain he could dish out. It was just that the metamorphosis he was going through was difficult and he still struggled with the person he was trying to become. He told himself he would get better at it.

The more he thought about it, the angrier he got. "I hate you," Hunter said. He meant to shout it but it came out low and raspy. He couldn't even hate right and this made him angrier still. He turned on his heel and headed back to his room, slamming the door behind him. *That's better*, he thought.

The next morning Hunter ignored his mother when she wished him a good day at school. This day, he didn't even bother to get on the school bus. Instead, he walked to the nearest city bus stop and waited. He was quickly rewarded with the arrival of a bus. Climbing on board, he put two quarters, the ones he had received from the stranger, in the coin machine and found a seat near the back of the bus.

The boy felt painfully alive, as though for the first time he was really free to make his own decisions. He didn't particularly care if they were good or not, only that they were *his* decisions. For the first time, he was not being guided by some specter that never really existed.

He stayed on the bus until it turned onto Federal Boulevard. He looked out the window, scanning each corner for the bench he had sat on the day before. As soon as it came into sight, he stood up and gave a quick tug on the cord over his head. A buzz went off in the front of the bus, and the driver glanced at him through the rearview mirror. The older man brought the bus to a stop in front of the bench, and Hunter walked forward.

"Whatcha doin' here boy?" asked the kindly man, his eyes and the tilt of his head expressing concern.

Hunter paused and looked out the door with one hand on the rail to steady himself. For the first time he realized he didn't even know why he had come. "I don't really know," he said quietly.

"Would you like me to take you back?"

"No. Back is definitely the wrong direction," he said. He lifted his chin with resolve as he jogged down the steps to the curb.

The bus driver shook his head slowly as he shut the doors, put the bus in gear and pulled back out into the busy traffic. Hunter watched it go before walking over to the bench and sitting down.

The young teen leaned back against the bench and stretched his arms out over the back, as though claiming the entire bench for himself. He looked around him and decided to just wait and see what came along. The man he met yesterday said he'd be back at eleven if Hunter wanted to talk. Hunter didn't really know if he wanted to talk but it was nice to have something on the schedule for the day. He set about memorizing each store, billboard and street sign.

It was well before eleven when he felt a hand on his shoulder that caused him to jump.

"Oh sorry, boy. I didn't mean to frighten you," said the man he had met the day before. The man walked around the bench and sat down next to Hunter, extending his hand. "I didn't even get your name yesterday. My name is Anthony. What's yours?" he asked with a friendly smile on his face that made Hunter feel safe and welcome.

"I'm Hunter."

"Nice English name. With your red hair and freckles I would have thought you were Irish."

Hunter blushed and ran his hands through his hair.

"So, you decided to come back. Why?" said Anthony, sounding genuinely curious.

"I don't know."

"Didn't have anything better to do, huh?"

"I guess not."

"Ya hungry?"

Hunter shrugged. "I'm okay."

"Well, I know you're okay, but I know a great donut shop just around the corner. How does that sound?"

It sounded great but Hunter only nodded briefly. The man apparently took the signal as a "yes," for he immediately stood up. Hunter followed, and the two of them walked around the corner and down Twenty-eighth. Half way down the block was a little hole-in-the-wall with a neon donut in the window blinking on and off. What the little shop lacked in ambiance it more than made up for in aroma the minute they stepped through the door. Donuts of all flavors and sizes filled the front case.

"Hey Anthony," said the girl behind the glass counter. "Good to see ya. Who's this ya got with ya?"

"This is my new friend Hunter. He's new around here. Hunter, this is Paula."

"Pleased ta meet cha," the young girl said with a friendly smile. "Anyone new ta the neighborhood gets their first donut free."

Hunter liked her immediately. "Thanks, ma'am."

"Ma'am? Ma'am is my mom. I'm way too young to be called ma'am," she laughed.

"Sorry. I didn't mean to insult you."

"Nah, don't worry 'bout it. It's nice ta see a young man what's been taught manners," and she gave Anthony a curt nod. "Take a lesson."

"Thanks a lot, Hunter. Now you're gettin' me in trouble with my homies!"

Hunter smiled. Teasing was not something he had grown up with and he wasn't quite sure how to respond.

Paula served them their donuts and tall cups of hot chocolate then scurried around the counter to clean off a table. "There ya go, boys. Enjoy yer donuts."

Hunter and Anthony sat down so that they were facing one another. Hunter looked down, embarrassed to make eye contact, and took a bite out of his donut.

Anthony watched him for his reaction. Pleased when he saw Hunter roll his eyes and smile, he said, "The best donuts anywhere."

Hunter, with frosting on his chin, nodded in agreement.

They ate in silence for a while. When Anthony finished his donut, he leaned back in his chair, brushing some white powdered sugar off his chin and looked at Hunter, his eyes intense. "So, you don't know why you came back. Do you want to tell me about it?"

Hunter looked out the window and listened to the debate going on his head. *Do I want to tell him? I don't even know him. What does he care, anyway?* He ran his hands through his hair then tugged gently on one ear.

Anthony had seen this before and just waited.

"I just need to start a new life, that's all,' Hunter finally responded, more to break the silence than for any other reason."

"A new life?'

"Yeah. Different than my old one. I need a new life that is real."

Anthony nodded. "I see. Maybe you could use a job."

Hunter's eyes lit up. He never expected at his age to find a job. "A job? Yeah! That would be great. But what kind of job could I get?"

"Well, I have a friend who could use an assistant."

Hunter's heart raced with excitement. *A job! A real job! My own money. That would be awesome!* He couldn't believe his luck. What were the chances of this happening?

Hunter could hardly sleep that night. *A job! A real job*. His mind raced with all the possibilities. Then a cold sweat covered his body and he began to panic. Anthony told him he would introduce him to his friend, a woman named Maria, tomorrow. What if she didn't like him? No...he would make sure she liked him.

His mind wandered back to dinner with his mother a few hours before. Once again, the school had called and asked where he was. He really didn't want his excitement spoiled so he decided to play the role of the repentant son. "I'm sorry, Mom. It won't happen again. I just needed to sort some things out in my head. I'm okay, now. You don't have to worry about me."

She smiled and gave him a hug and a kiss on the forehead.

Mothers can be so gullible, he thought, not feeling the least bit guilty. He was pleased that he was progressing in his lying ability. *I must have inherited that from her.*

CHAPTER 3

Running Away

THE MORNING DID NOT go at all as expected. Instead of giving him a wave "good-bye" at the door, Melody put on her coat and walked out with him.

"Where're you goin', Mom?" he asked, his eyes wide with surprise.

"I'm coming to school with you," she said as she flashed him a sweet smile.

"What? You've got to be kidding. You can't do that!" he shouted. He felt the blood rush to his ears and his heart start to pound.

"No, I'm not and yes, I can," she responded, keeping her voice low.

"Mom, this is ridiculous. I told you I was fine. I'm all better now. You don't have to babysit me."

"I'm not babysitting you. I just want to help you."

"Well, this is not helping. Geesh. How embarrassing. My mom coming to school with me. You're treating me like I'm in Kindergarten!" He felt perspiration bead up on his forehead.

The whole way to school his mind raced. What was he going to do? He had to meet Anthony. If he didn't show up, Anthony would think he didn't want the job. By the time his mother pulled into the visitor parking, he had come up with a plan.

"Well, let's get this over with," he said as he got out of the car, trying to keep his voice and demeanor calm.

"So, what's our first class?" asked his mother cheerfully.

"Algebra II," he responded. He stomped into the school ahead of her. Melody hurried to keep up with him as he dodged between the kids in the crowded hallway. Hunter ignored the stares and not so subtle smirks from the other teens.

Hunter slipped into the classroom and slid into the seat closest to the door. He hid his face as his mother found a chair in the back of the room. Mr. Lancaster walked in and, of course, noticed the guest immediately. "Well, welcome. Who do we have visiting today? Does this mother belong to any of you kids?" He waited, looking over the room with expectation and a cheery smile on his face.

"That's Hunter's mom," piped up one of the kids who Hunter, before this day, counted as a friend.

Snickers were heard around the room.

Hunter kept his head down, staring through the top of the desk.

"Well, Hunter, would you be so kind as to introduce your mother to us?" asked Mr. Lancaster.

"This is my mother," Hunter said without looking up.

"Oh my. I'm sure you can do better than that. Please escort her up to the front of the room and introduce her properly."

Hunter's face matched his hair as he walked to the back of the room. "Come on, Mom," he whispered through clenched teeth. Once in the front of the room, he looked out the window instead of at the class. He knew what they were doing...he didn't need to see it.

"This is my Mom, Melody Mitchell. She is visiting my classes today."

"Welcome, Mrs. Mitchell," said Mr. Lancaster. "We are pleased to have you with us."

"Thank you," said Melody with a smile. She shook the teacher's hand before returning to her seat.

Hunter slithered back to his desk but only for a moment before he raised his hand. "Mr. Lancaster, with all the excitement of having my mom here, I completely forgot to stop at my locker to get my homework. May I have a hall pass, please?"

With Hunter's mother sitting right there, Mr. Lancaster had to be nice. "Sure," he said.

Hunter grabbed the pass, dashed out the classroom door, down the hall and out the front doors. By the time his mother came out of the classroom to look for him, he was already on the city bus headed for Federal Boulevard.

As the bus drove down Federal and

neared the corner of Twenty-eighth, Hunter looked out the window and saw Anthony walking away, a young woman beside him. He pounded on the window as they drove past. Anthony looked up, saw Hunter through the glass and waved. He and the young woman turned around and headed back to the bus stop, arriving just after Hunter got off the bus.

"Hey, buddy," called Anthony. "I thought you weren't coming."

"Of course I was coming. I just had to take care of some things at home first," said Hunter, trying to sound grown up in front of his prospective future boss. "Is this Maria?" he said while extending his hand.

As he shook her hand, Hunter examined the young woman. She was short and a bit plump. She had long, thick, black hair that fell in waves around a pretty face. Her eyes were heavily outlined in black eyeliner and her full lips were thickly covered with glossy red lipstick. She wore a pink uniform with the symbol of a well-known hotel on the pocket. She looked at him with unconcealed skepticism. "He's awfully young, don't you think, Anthony?"

"Young, yes. But eager to learn, aren't you boy?" said Anthony while patting him on the back.

"You bet I am! And I am very trustworthy." He almost added: "You can ask my Mom," but the way he had been acting lately, especially leaving her at the school, would probably quell any recommendations from her. So, he just left it there.

"Have you told him what the job is?" she asked.

Hunter was getting a little irritated that she was carrying on this conversation as though he couldn't hear or speak for himself.

"Anthony said you need an assistant," Hunter said.

Maria turned and looked at him. Then she shook her head. "No. He's too young."

Anthony grabbed her arm and turned her to face him. "Look, Maria. I know he's young but he's perfect. He's clean-cut and as pure as the driven snow." Grabbing Hunter's chin he added, "Just look at those freckles!"

This made Maria smile and, for the first time in his life, Hunter was actually glad he had freckles. "Okay," she said. "You might have a point there. But you train him. He obviously doesn't know the first thing about our business." She turned and started walking down the street.

Hunter felt his heart leap for joy as his mouth broke into a broad smile. "Thanks, Maria. You won't regret it!"

Maria turned half way back. "I just hope *you* don't, boy."

Anthony led the way down the street to a sandwich shop and ordered their food to go. He walked to a bench in front of an antique store with Hunter right behind him. He said very little until they finished their lunch.

"So, Hunter, my boy," he began with a fatherly tone in his voice, at least the tone Hunter once imagined his father's would have. "You need to start standing on your own two feet. You need to start taking control of your own life instead of having others run your life for you. Is that right?"

"That's for sure," Hunter said with conviction.

"The job I have for you will help you do just that. It will be quite easy for a clever boy such as you."

Hunter smiled and nodded. Here was someone who appreciated him for who he was.

"Now, listen carefully to what I'm going to tell you. Maria works for that hotel over there and several others as well." Anthony motioned with his chin toward a well-known hotel standing kitty-corner across the street. "She has a very responsible position. She is in charge of cleaning all of the rooms on the west wing of the fourth floor every morning. She is also in charge of several other maids on different floors and in different hotels around downtown."

Hunter nodded, not having any idea where this was going.

"The hotels offer a free breakfast to their guests. So, every morning, before checking out or going about their business, the people leave their rooms to go downstairs to eat. While they're gone, Maria needs an assistant who can go into the rooms and gather up a few things."

Hunter's eyes popped wide open as realization of what he was saying struck him like a two by four across the face. "You mean steal stuff?"

"Well, not a lot of stuff. Just a few things."

"I've never stolen anything in my life! I can't do that!" Hunter responded, his heart pounding within him and sweat beading up on his forehead.

"Why not?"

"Well...I just can't."

"Okay. Maybe I had you pegged wrong. Maybe you really just want to stay a momma's boy and never make something of yourself."

Anger well up inside him. He clenched his fists and pounded his thigh. "I'm *not* a momma's boy. I can do what I want. I just don't want to steal stuff."

"Afraid you'd get caught?" said Anthony, perhaps seeing a chink in Hunter's armor.

"Well, that's part of it."

"Of course it is. But you won't get caught here. This is the easiest job ever. As soon as they leave their rooms and get on the elevator, Maria lets you in the room with her card. You run in, shuffle through some stuff, grab anything you find that can be sold, such as cell phones or lap-tops, or even cash or jewelry, and you are out of there. Five minutes max. The people are just eating waffles and drinking orange juice downstairs. They never even know what's happening. Nobody gets hurt, and we get rich."

Hunter looked down at the ground and shook his head, his heart still pounding wildly. His hands felt cold and clammy, and he rubbed them on his pants, the rough denim warming them and soaking up the moisture. His thoughts turned to his dad. He smirked. Sure, he could do this, he told himself. It was in his blood. Hadn't his mother always told him she wanted him to grow up to be just like his dad? This would certainly show her that he could. But steal other people's stuff? Could he really do that? How far was this metamorphosis going to go? How far would he let it go?

Anthony watched the boy closely as the teen mulled over the proposition. He waited patiently, obviously not wanting to push too hard and run the risk of pushing Hunter away.

Several minutes passed. The noise from the traffic on the street ebbed and flowed with the changing of the traffic signal. People on the sidewalk strolled past in friendly conversation or hustled by in silence. All were oblivious to the internal war taking place within the young teen as he sat hunched on the antique bench set artistically in front of the store.

At last, Hunter slowly raised his head and looked boldly into Anthony's eyes. "I'll do it once just to see how it goes. Got it? Just once. If I don't like it, that's it. No more."

Anthony's mouth lifted into half a smile as he extended his hand. "It's a deal."

CHAPTER 4

Becoming a Thief

ANTHONY PUT HUNTER UP for the night at his place. Anthony lived on the top floor of an old home that had been converted into two apartments. It smelled of last night's fried fish mixed with a cat's litter box that needed changing. The furniture was nice enough for a single guy, but it appeared that it hadn't seen a dust cloth its whole life. Some dirty dishes were scattered around the room with remnants of past meals that the cat had not chosen to clean up. Hunter found himself surprised by a small shrine of sorts sitting on the fireplace mantel. A picture of Jesus hung on the wall and a red glass candleholder had been placed reverently in front of it, a small flame making the red glass glow.

Anthony baked a frozen pizza for dinner then challenged Hunter to a video game. Hunter's inexperience playing video games coupled with being distracted meant he was an easy target, even when Anthony tried to go easy on him. Hunter's nerves were on edge, and he couldn't keep his hands from shaking. He also had a hard time concentrating on the game. His mind jumped back and forth between what tomorrow would bring and what his mother must be going through. The latter thought kept popping into his mind even though he did everything he could to stop it. It was like trying to suppress a cough...no matter how hard he tried, it kept coming back.

Anthony brought Hunter a blanket and pillow and set him up on the living room couch. He said goodnight and disappeared into the bedroom, leaving Hunter alone with his thoughts. Hunter lay on the couch and stared up at the ceiling. He watched the flickering light from the shrine's candle that Anthony had left burning in the red votive candleholder dance around the ceiling. He glanced over at the glowing red glass, consciously avoiding looking at the picture of Jesus, and watched it pulse like a beating heart...his beating heart. *What am I doing here?* he asked himself over and over until sleep finally overtook him.

While Hunter ate, played and worried at Anthony's apartment, Melody was at home in a condition that can best be described as terrified. When she returned home to an empty house, she was originally filled with anger, then overcome with worry, then consumed with panic. She called everyone she could think of and everyone that everyone she called could think of. No one had seen or heard from Hunter. She started driving around, up and down the streets, extending her search farther and farther. As it got darker outside, so did her insides. Once the sun set, she called the police.

Anthony woke Hunter before the sun was up by shaking his shoulder. "Up and at 'em. It's a work day for you. Maria wants you on her floor by 7:00. Go get cleaned up while I fix us some breakfast."

Hunter began moving as though on auto-pilot. He didn't think about what lay ahead. He just went through his usual morning routine...shower...get dressed...eat breakfast. All the same except for one notable exception: he had to put on the same pants and shirt he had worn the day before. He ate his breakfast cereal without saying a word, without even looking at Anthony.

Anthony appeared to sense Hunter's discomfort and, perhaps, even felt a bit sorry for the young boy. He sat down beside him. "Hey, you don't have to do this. You can still back out if you want. I just wanted to give you a chance to make something of yourself."

Hunter shook his head but didn't look away from the cornflake that was floating alone on the milk. "I'm okay," he said softly as he used his spoon to push the cornflake under the surface.

The two cohorts were out of the apartment by 6:30 in the morning. Anthony walked down the street with a jaunty step, whistling a country-western song, as though he hadn't a care in the world. Hunter shuffled along behind him, his head down, his shoulders slumped. He could feel the veins in his forehead pulsing with the beating of his heart. He didn't look to the right or the left but kept his feet stepping on Anthony's shadow as they moved up one block then another. After twenty minutes, they arrived at the front doors of the hotel.

"Here we are, Hunter," Anthony said, shoving a black backpack into his hands. "Oh, and remember, if anything goes wrong, I've never met you," he added as he pushed Hunter through the front doors.

"Some friend you are," Hunter wanted to say but didn't. Instead he walked sheepishly across the lobby and up to the elevators. He pushed the up button and waited. When the doors opened, a young couple walked out and the thought crossed Hunter's mind: *I wonder if that's whose room I'll be in.* With no way of knowing, he pushed the thought out of his head and stepped into the elevator.

The doors opened on the fourth floor and Hunter stepped out into a nearly empty and very long hallway. Turning to his right, he noticed that the maid cart was sitting several doorways down. He hesitated for a moment. Then anger welled up inside of him as he thought of his father. His resolve strengthened. "Yeah, Mom, I'm going to grow up to be just like him!" he said under his breath. The anger turned to conviction as he stomped toward the cart.

Maria came out of one of the rooms just as Hunter reached the cart. She glanced from side to side toward both ends of the long hallway then pulled him into the room she was cleaning. "Wait in here. These people have checked out, so you will be safe. I'll come back to get you when I have the right target." She went out the door and shut it, leaving Hunter alone in the room. Suddenly the door opened and Maria stuck her head around the door. "And don't get anything dirty. I've already cleaned that room!" The door shut again.

Hunter paced back and forth. He contemplated turning on the T.V. but thought better of it. He hoped he wouldn't be there long. His stomach was churning and he wished he hadn't eaten any breakfast.

He really wasn't there long, it just seemed that way. He jumped when he heard the lock on the door unlatch and the door open. "Come on. Now!" he heard Maria say. He hustled through the door and into the hall. Maria led the way without looking at him. She hurried down the hall, past several doors, finally stopping at one. Looking both ways to make sure the hallway was empty, she inserted her card and pushed down on the door handle.

The door opened silently. Maria motioned toward the opening with her chin and whispered, "Remember, just look for anything you think could be sold. Of course, cash is good too. No more than five minutes, understand?"

Hunter felt sick, but he nodded his head and entered the room. The door shut behind him.

It took nearly a minute for his eyes to adjust to the near darkness. The dim light coming through a tiny gap in the drapes that covered the window provided the only illumination.

"Okay, I can do this...just this once," he said softly.

He began looking on the counter and desktops, then moved to the bedside table. On the table were a watch and a cell phone. He grabbed them and stuffed them into his backpack. He moved to the suitcases. One lay open on the floor. He shuffled through it as he felt sweat beading up on his forehead and rolling down his chest. It felt like he was violating someone else's personal stuff looking through the suitcase...more than just picking up a cell phone off the table. In one of the pockets, he found a roll of cash. He didn't take time to count it before shoving it in the backpack. Not finding anything else, he moved to the closed suitcase sitting on the stand. He quietly opened it.

It took him just a moment to find the jewelry. Sitting on one end of the suitcase was a dark blue velvet box. He picked up the box and opened it. Inside were several necklaces and bracelets that appeared, to his untrained eye, to be covered with diamonds. He quickly snapped the box shut and added it to his collection.

Just then, there was a knock on the door. His heart stopped, and he froze in place. He heard the card unlatch the lock and he glanced around in an effort to find a place to hide. To his immeasurable relief, he saw Maria poke her head in the room. "Time's up. Get out now!"

Relief overflowing, he headed for the door. At that moment, his eye caught sight of a briefcase sitting on the floor beside the bed. He stopped. Bending down, he unzipped the case and pulled out a laptop computer. Working it into the largest pocket of the backpack, he headed out of the room and down the hall toward the elevators without even looking for Maria. But, he could feel her eyes on the back of his head, and it made a shiver run through his body.

He pushed the button on the elevator and stood impatiently in front of the shiny golden doors until he could endure waiting no longer. Turning to his right, he headed for the exit sign that marked the stairway. He opened the fire door and dashed down the three flights of stairs to the lobby. Without looking at anyone, he hurried to the front doors, his backpack weighing him down as though he were Atlas carrying the entire world on his shoulders.

As soon as he stepped out into the bright sunlight, Anthony was by his side. The young man grabbed the backpack with one hand and Hunter's arm with the other. He pulled the boy down the street quickly, not saying a word. That was fine with Hunter. He didn't feel like talking anyway. If the truth be told, he felt most like vomiting.

They reached the corner and, without looking in either direction, stepped off the curb. Just as they did so, a single *whoop* from a siren sounded out and a police car screeched to a stop, blocking their path. Hunter froze in place. Anthony let go of his arm and turned to run. In a split second, two policemen jumped out of the car and surrounded him.

"Not so fast, mister. You're coming with us," said the taller of the two officers.

Without further resistance, Anthony climbed in the back seat of the police car. Hunter noticed that he did so with an air of familiarity, as if he had done this a thousand times before. Hunter didn't know if he had and knew he would never ask. He didn't really want to know. The freckled-faced teen just ducked his head and slid in beside him, sitting as Anthony sat, feet flat, hands on his knees.

CHAPTER 5

The Mustang

THE LITTLE MUSTANG MARE noticed a soft *whomp, whomp, whomp* sound, coming from somewhere off in the distance. She twitched her ears back and forth trying to locate the sound while she kept her top lip wiggling back and forth, sifting through the sandy soil, searching for something edible. The spring rains had been sparse and the summer thunderstorms had been stingy when it came to providing any water. By this time in the fall there was little to eat on the high plains.

The dun colored mare with black legs and a thick and tangled black mane and tail was very thin, but not as thin as the mares that had foals at their sides. Her little colt, her pride and joy, had been killed by a pack of coyotes a few months earlier. She still suffered with grief, a grief that tore at her heart every day. The tears on her flesh from the coyotes' teeth had healed, but not the wounds on the heart from her failure to protect her son. Perhaps they never would.

The *whomp, whomp, whomp* sound continued to get louder, causing the mare to lift her head and seek out the alpha mare. The lead mare was standing tall and alert, her neck arched and her head up. Her ears were pricked sharply forward as she stared toward the direction that the sun sets, though it was far from that time of day.

A strange shape appeared in the sky, looking something like an enormous insect. As the odd creature grew larger, the sound it made grew louder. The horses were gripped with fear. The *whomp, whomp* sound that echoed off the northern cliffs changed to a chopping sound and the insect turned into a flying monster heading straight toward them. All of the mares and foals panicked and began to scatter. But the strong herd instinct within each horse took over and drew them back together as a magnet attracts metal. They were soon running together, side-by-side or nose to tail, with the alpha mare in the lead.

The monster flew over their heads and past the herd. Once in front, it spun around in the air so that it was facing them. This caused the wild horses to change course and go back in the direction they had come. Suddenly, from out of the arroyo that cut into the prairie on the west, four humans on horses appeared. They split into two pairs and ran toward the oncoming mustangs. With the monster insect behind them, the alpha mare dashed straight ahead, between the two sets of riders. The dun-colored mare stayed right beside her left flank, running stride for stride with her, as though connected shoulder to hip. They dashed down into the arroyo. Some of the humans on horseback blocked the ravine to the right so the entire herd turned south.

The mares were already winded and sweating profusely from both exertion and anxiety. Regardless, they kept running. Clouds of dust flew up behind them, scattered quickly by the whirling, noisy monster pushing them onward. The *chop, chop, chop* sound above them easily drowned out the pounding of the mustangs' hooves, their snorts and whinnies as well as the shouts of the humans as they drove the mustangs forward.

At the end of the arroyo, several portable metal fence panels had been set up creating a large pen. Once the little herd of mustangs got to the end of the arroyo, the alpha mare entered the portable corral and stopped. Her followers did as well. She looked frantically from side to side, searching in vain for an escape route. As the last wild horse entered the enclosure, two panels were quickly brought together by a human on the ground, closing off the opening. The horses were trapped.

The humans whooped and hollered, celebrating their success. This had been an easier-than-usual round-up for the Bureau of Land Management employees. No one had been hurt, neither human nor animal. That was always a relief.

Assigned with the task of managing the herds of wild horses on BLM land to a level that the land could support, this had been a busy year. The drought had left little forage for the horses, and many were literally starving to death. These mares and foals that were now running frantically around the pen, neighing, kicking and bucking, would probably not survive the cold winter if left on their own, particularly those nursing mothers with foals at their sides. The cowboys were all horse-lovers and they wanted to do their best for this band of wild horses. They intended to find homes for them where the horses would be well cared for.

The herd was hot, tired, hungry and thirsty. The cowboys brought them hay and water. Soon they were all drinking and eating, following the alpha mare's example.

With food finally in her stomach, the little dun mare took the time to walk around the perimeter of the pen, looking out on the prairie that had once been her home. She wondered if she would ever run free across those lands again. At one point in the fence, her view was blocked by a strange looking object. It looked somewhat like a huge rock with slits in it. She had no idea what it could be but since it was not moving or making any noise, she decided it was harmless enough.

Once the sun set, the temperature dropped quickly. The horses continued to mill around the pen beneath the countless stars. Sometime, during the deepest, darkest part of the moonless night, the alpha mare lifted her head and whinnied. Her call was answered by another whinny from somewhere in the darkness. The sound of a single set of pounding hooves was heard getting louder. All of the mares and foals stopped and waited. Suddenly, the stallion of the herd appeared at the barrier, having run down the same gorge the herd had come down during the day. He stopped at the fence and reared high in the air. He threw his head back and let out a loud screaming neigh, easily communicating his displeasure that his mares had been taken from him. He whirled and began kicking with both feet at the metal bars of the fence panels. The mares and foals began running around the pen, frightened by the loud crashing noise the stallion was making.

The crashing and banging had gone on for several minutes when, suddenly, it stopped. A loud pain-laden scream was emitted from deep within the stallion. One of his kicks had resulted in a hind leg getting wedged between two metal panels. He struggled to free himself but doing so only succeeded in tearing the skin and muscle below the hock down to the bone. He began bleeding profusely and the pain became unbearable.

The mares stopped running and turned to face the stallion. Slowly, the alpha mare walked up to where the stallion was stuck. As she approached, he struggled violently again, trying to free himself, but to no avail. She nickered softly, and he stopped and looked at her, his eyes filled with a mixture of pain and sadness. She reached her muzzle through the bars of the fence and rubbed his heaving sides, trying to calm him. The mare stood with him throughout the night, rubbing him and nickering to him, as the life-blood drained from his once proud body and soaked into the soil in front of the mare's hooves.

By the time the cowboys returned in the morning, the stallion was dead.

The cowboys opened a panel that covered the odd looking object the dun mare had noticed the day before. With the fencing gone, the strange thing now looked like a long, narrow cave that came to a dead end. Light poured in from the openings along the side but the ceiling that ran along the top kept it rather dark. With shouts and whirling ropes, the little band of wild horses was forced into the cave.

As they entered, their hooves beat on the wooden floorboards and the contraption shook and vibrated. With very little room to move around, the horses stood together, their sweating bodies pressed up against one another. They snorted and stomped and waited to see what was going to happen next in this strange new object in which they were trapped.

They didn't have to wait long before a roaring sound reached their ears, sending a new level of panic through the herd. The bravest dared to look out between the bars that lined the sides of the cave. The little dun mare was one of those. She saw several humans milling around outside the cave, and she watched as they put their horses into some sort of container that looked like a smaller version of the cave they were in. These horses simply walked in and didn't seem the least bit frightened. This was strange to her, something she couldn't understand, having been raised to fear nearly everything in order to survive.

With another loud roar, the cave started to move, causing a new wave of fear to pulsate through the herd. Some of the mares struggled to keep their footing as they worked their way through the trembling bodies to find their foals. Other than that, the horses just stood where they were, trying to keep their balance as the odd cave-like apparatus was pulled across the bumpy terrain.

CHAPTER 6

Promise Ranch

THE SHIMMERING IMAGES SPARKLED and evaporated on the black, snake-like road ahead. It was hot and dry, typical of the Arizona desert. Hunter and his grandfather had been on the road for nearly nine hours. Driving straight into the sun was taking its toll on the old man. Hunter slept most of the time, or at least pretended to. He didn't want to talk. He sat touching the door, his head pressed against the window, with clenched thoughts. His grandfather's attempts at conversation were met with silence or, at the most, grunts. So the old man gave up trying.

As they drove along, Hunter's mind replayed his day in court over and over. He saw his mother's sad eyes as she set her jaw in an obvious attempt to be brave. He saw the judge with his stern face, his mouth set in a firm line. He saw his grandfather pleading for mercy on his behalf.

Images.

Brutal images.

When Hunter stood before the juvenile court judge, his grandfather stepped up with an offer of a solution. He had found a great ranch in Arizona that took in "at-risk boys." He offered to pay the hefty monthly tuition in an attempt to save his grandson. The judge had agreed that this would be the best way to help Hunter, and the deal was struck. Hunter sat in the courtroom silently, a sullen scowl on his face as these men discussed, and decided upon, his fate.

At-risk? At-risk of what? Becoming the kind of man I have always been told to become...just like my father? Hunter thought.

Somewhere in the back of his mind, he knew he should be grateful to his grandfather, but if he was, he certainly wasn't going to show it. He knew now that he was born to be a trouble-maker and that's what he would be. His grandfather could waste his money if he wanted - fine! But that wasn't going to change a thing.

Late in the afternoon, the car turned off the two-lane, nearly deserted desert highway and passed under an attractive rustic-looking sign that read: "Promise Ranch." The tires of the car bounced violently as they drove over the cattle guard, a series of pipes over a trench extending across the dirt driveway. They are designed to keep cattle and horses from crossing over and getting in the road. Hunter looked out the window at the land around him. No lush, verdant garden here. All the boy could see was weeds and rocks and dirt, punctuated with an occasional pinon pine. To Hunter, they had just entered the middle of nowhere. Why anyone would live out here he had no idea. Nor did he want to find out.

Promise Ranch was an island surrounded by a vast sea of federal lands and Indian reservations. Long held in private hands, its last owner, a wealthy entrepreneur, had established a foundation to ensure that Promise Ranch would be a home for teenage boys for as long as the sun rose and set over the desert ranchland.

Hunter's grandpa drove down the dirt road until they arrived at a large log ranch house. The expansive building was designed with architecture that made it appear much more rustic than it really was. A plump woman was waiting for them on the covered front porch. Her hands nearly dissolved into the rolls of fat on her hips; her eyes nearly disappeared into her cheeks as she squinted toward the retreating sun. She waved at them and smiled.

"I've been expecting you," she said as she bent over and peered in the driver's side window, looking past Hunter's grandfather and giving the boy a wink of her eye. "You must be William Mitchell," she said, looking back at the older man.

"Yes, ma'am," responded Hunter's grandfather as he extended his hand.

Taking his hand warmly in both of hers, she peeked through the window once again and looked over at Hunter who was now staring straight ahead. "And you must be Hunter. I'm Mrs. Fowler," she said. Ignoring Hunter's rudeness she added, "I'm so happy to have you join our ranch family."

Grandfather and grandson silently unloaded the trunk of the car. Missing from Hunter's bags was his violin. He had adamantly refused to bring it along, even with his mother's pleading.

Mrs. Fowler went into the ranch house to get some lemonade, promising to cool them off before showing Hunter to his cabin.

Boy and grandfather stepped up on the porch that spanned the front of the large log cabin. To the right of the door, someone had placed a six-foot tall wooden carving of a cowboy. At one time, it had been painted in bright colors, giving it an almost clown-like appearance. But the sun had left its mark and now the carving was covered with cracks, and faded and peeling paint. It was quite old, but it had an odd, friendly sort of smile that had stood the test of time. It was the smile that served to welcome visitors.

Hunter sat down on one of the rocking chairs that had been placed on the front porch to the side of the wooden cowboy. The boards that covered the porch creaked and groaned as he rapidly rocked back and forth. The air smelled of warm rain and rotting grasses. Flashes of lightning vibrated across the sky to the north. The thunder reached his ears in whispers.

Mrs. Fowler returned carrying a tray with tall glasses of lemonade and a plate of peanut butter cookies. Hunter refused to mention that those were his favorite.

"How long have you been at Promise Ranch," asked Hunter's grandfather, trying to make polite conversation.

"Oh, I guess it must be goin' on ten years now," she said with a twinkle in her eye. If truth be told, Betsy Fowler had been at the ranch for thirty-four years. But she had a habit of refusing to acknowledge the passing of time and her own aging.

Having been widowed at a young age, she came to the ranch to escape her own pain. She felt immediately at home on the ranch. She found endless entertainment just watching the horses and the cowboys. She felt like she was free in the wide-open spaces and the mountains that bordered the valley to the north. She marveled at the gorgeous sunrises and sunsets. She felt a thrill pass through her as she watched the thunderheads roll in, bringing lightning and thunder and hard rains. Most of all, she was drawn to the boys who came to heal, or pay their just dues, or to simply "get their head on straight," as she would say. She really didn't care why they were at the ranch. She just tried to love them with all the strength her spirit could muster. And that was a lot.

No one seemed to know what to say next so an awkward silence hung in the air. Hunter's grandpa swirled the ice cubes around in his glass while Betsy took a sip of her lemonade. "Well, Hunter, I am very happy that you are here," she finally repeated.

Hunter didn't look up and didn't respond.

"Son, you were spoken to," said his grandpa.

Hunter rolled his eyes, and then said, "Yeah, well, I'm not glad to be here."

Betsy smiled warmly. She reached over and patted the boy's knee. "I understand. But you will find that this is a healing place."

"I don't need any healing," he said as he jerked his knee away from her hand.

Hunter's grandpa looked over at him. It hurt to see the pain in the boy's eyes, and he really didn't understand, exactly, why it was there. Sure, he knew the trouble had started when his father had appeared out of nowhere.

But just why he had reacted in such an extreme manner, the old man could not figure out. One thing he did know, however, was that something inside the boy had died.

Betsy spent the next several minutes going over some of the ranch rules and a typical day's schedule. Every boy had daily chores. A home school curriculum was planned for each boy and that would be done on weekday afternoons. He was expected to keep his cabin clean and do his own laundry. A counselor would meet with him as often as needed or desired. And there was no swearing allowed...ever.

The business complete, Betsy led Hunter and his grandpa around the main ranch house to where a row of rustic cabins sat side-by-side, as though keeping one another company. They stepped up on the wooden porch of the third cabin. The name over the door read "M Lazy C." Betsy pulled open the screen door and pushed open the door to the cabin.

Once inside, Hunter could see that the cabin had two beds, one on either side of the room. At the foot of each bed was a dresser. The bed to the right appeared to be occupied. A cowboy hat adorned the top of one of the bedposts and a denim jacket was tossed casually across the colorful patchwork quilt. The quilt was created in a pattern of plaids, polka-dots and paisley in shades of green, gold and brown. It reminded Hunter of the one airplane trip he had taken. Gazing out the window of the plane, he had marveled at the way the farmers' fields formed a pattern that looked like a patchwork quilt comforting the earth.

Hunter's eye moved over to the dresser. On top of the dresser, sending out a bluish glow, was an illuminated, bubbling fish tank. The water plants swayed from side to side while the fish swam lazily back and forth, befitting the name of the cabin.

Motioning to that side of the room, Betsy said, "This side is Julius's. He'll be your roommate. You are going to get along right fine with him. He's a gentle giant if I've ever seen one." Turning to the other side of the room she added, "And this is your space." She plopped her large body down on the bed and patted the bedspread. "I want you to know that I made these quilts myself. They will keep you nice and warm during our cold desert nights." She smiled warmly at Hunter but didn't get much of a response. No matter. She had dealt with this type of behavior before. She couldn't blame him, or any of the boys. It must be awfully frightening to come so far from home and be all alone. She knew how to be patient.

"Julius, you say?" Hunter's grandpa added. "Where's he now."

"Out doin' his chores or playin' with his horse I 'spect. He'll be back in time for dinner, though. You can be sure of that. Julius never wants to miss a meal," she chuckled. "I'd like to think it's my fine cookin' that he likes but I think any food will do for Julius." She laughed heartily. The older man smiled. Hunter turned and gazed out the window.

The morning sunlight poured in the south windows in long shafts, lighting the dancing specks of dust. Hunter slowly opened his eyes. It took him just a minute to remember where he was. When the realization came rushing back to him it brought the anger with it. He began pounding the mattress with his fist.

Hunter had met his cabin mate, Julius, the night before. Julius was a tall, muscular black kid, originally from Chicago, now Salt Lake City. He had an earthy sort of confidence about him that Hunter was instinctively drawn to but he forced himself to put up a wall. Julius tried to be nice to Hunter, tried to make him feel welcome. But Hunter would have none of it. He didn't want to be friends with this kid, nice as he was. He didn't want to let his guard down even for a minute. He had decided to be miserable and miserable he would be!

The sounds of men shouting and horses neighing reached his ears and Hunter realized that was what had awakened him. He stopped pounding his fist, turned his head and looked over at Julius's bed. It was empty, the covers hastily thrown over the pillow. The cowboy hat was gone from its perch on the bedpost. His eyes rested for a moment on the fish tank, watching the fish swim back and forth, back and forth. As he watched, he listened to the sounds coming from somewhere outside. Whoops and hollers from men continued as they mixed with whinnies and neighs from horses.

Hunter threw back the handmade quilt and swung his feet out of the bed. He stood up and stretched. The bed was not the best he had ever been in but, if forced, he'd have to admit it wasn't all that bad either. He hurried over to the door, opened it and stepped out on the wooden porch that extended across the front of his cabin. The shouts and neighs that first awakened him were still filling the air, and Hunter could see a cloud of peach-colored dust rising up from the end of the row of cabins...from where the barn and horse pens were located. Curious, Hunter returned to the cabin and dressed quickly.

Hurrying out of the cabin, he let the screen door bang loudly behind him. He walked quickly toward the sounds and the dust. When he rounded the last cabin, he stopped. Ahead of him he immediately recognized his roommate, Julius, mounted on a small brown and white paint horse. The tall, lanky boy's legs hung well past the horse's barrel. Julius's cowboy hat shaded the dark skin of the boy's face as he swung a rope over his head in an attempt to herd a band of a dozen other horses.

Another rider was helping Julius but this was a much older man. From what Hunter could see through the dust cloud, this man must have been in his forties or fifties. The skin of his face looked like tanned leather and was lined with wrinkles. The cracks and crevasses on his well-worn skin did nothing to conceal the sparkle in his eyes, however. He was slim in build but Hunter could see that, beneath his plaid, cotton shirt, his arms were bulging with muscles. He spoke softly to Julius, giving him instructions. The man's name was Charlie Perkins but everyone called him "Smokey." His friends described him as a man who was hard headed and soft hearted. His soft heart was most often revealed when he worked with animals and kids.

"Move to the left and cut off that one big brown mare....good. Now, swing your rope over your head and move the whole herd around the pen away from the gate."

This went on for several minutes while a long, gray horse trailer was pulled away, and a man, or boy, Hunter couldn't tell which, quickly shut the gate to the circular paddock.

"Great work, Julius. Let's get them some food and water then head to the lodge for Betsy's breakfast."

As Julius and the cowboy dismounted, the herd moved to the far side of the corral...as far away from these men and their sold-out horses as they could get. Hunter walked quietly to the fence where he could be close to the herd. He stepped up on the bottom rail and leaned forward over the top.

One small dun-colored mare with a thick black mane turned her entire body toward him. The mare's eyes held him spellbound for more than a minute. As Hunter looked into the large, warm, brown eyes, it seemed as though she was sending him a distinct message: "I know you. I know you down to the core." Hunter closed his eyes. When he opened them, the mare had moved off to join the other mustangs. *Perhaps it was just my over-active imagination*, he thought.

But the brief exchange had been picked up by Smokey, who had watched the new boy approach. When it came to horses and boys, there wasn't much that the old cowboy missed. He stepped up to the fence beside Hunter and rested his arm on the top rail. "I could use your help with that mare if you're up to it."

Hunter straightened and stepped down from the fence. He rolled his eyes. "I don't do horses. If they don't have a motor and four tires," he said, thinking of the ATV's on his grandpa's farm, "I don't ride 'em."

The cowboy shrugged his shoulders and turned to look at the little herd of new mustangs he had just adopted from the Bureau of Land Management. "Well, that's quite a few horses and somebody's gonna have to help me. Might as well be you." He stuck out his hand, "I'm Smokey. You must be the new boy, Hunter. I'm pleased to meet you." Hunter put his hands in his pockets. Smokey shrugged, dropped his hand and turned on his well-worn heel. As he walked away, he had a smile on his face. Smokey prided himself on being able to read teenage boys as well as he could read horses.

With a whoop and holler, a rope sailed over Hunter's head and tightened around his chest, pinning his arms to his side. "Hey...what the heck!" Hunter exclaimed as he turned around. "What do ya think yer doin'!" he yelled.

At the other end of the rope stood Julius, laughing with delight. "Hey Smokey! I caught myself a young steer!"

Hunter, his jaw clenched and his face red with both anger and embarrassment, peeled the rope down and stepped out of it.

"Let's go get some grub, Hunter," said Julius, clearly pleased with himself. He pulled the rope toward him and wound it in even loops as they walked toward the large log ranch house. Hunter went along reluctantly, still fuming at being lassoed.

The welcoming aroma of bacon wafted on the gentle breeze toward them. Hunter felt his stomach growl and his anger subside a bit, softened by the welcoming fragrance of a hot breakfast. Food does that to a boy.

As they entered the great room Hunter saw that several boys of various ages, sizes and races were already feasting on Betsy's culinary creations. Hunter looked from one face to the next. They all had the fresh faces created by outdoor work. They smiled and laughed as they exchanged a happy banter back and forth.

Hunter let his eyes take in the surroundings. At the end of the room was a tall, stone fireplace, extending to the ceiling. On this warm desert morning, there were no flames on the logs that sat in wait. The walls on both sides of the massive fireplace were decorated with a collection of cowboy hats and branding irons, artfully arranged over the log walls. The long side of the room directly in front of him was all windows. Below the windows were desks with computers. He guessed that this was where they did their schoolwork. To his left were several doors, one of which was open revealing a large kitchen. He could see Mrs. Fowler bustling around. Overhead, log beams formed an artistic pattern as they supported the heavy roof of the lodge. It was at once both magnificent and cozy.

Julius guided Hunter up to the side of the room where platters of food rested on tables covered with red and white checked tablecloths. The food was plentiful and, judging from the aroma, all had a bit of southwestern spice to it.

"Eat up, Hunter," said Julius as he dished himself up a huge pile of scrambled eggs and biscuits. "You don't have to worry about getting fat around here. There's plenty of work to do. We have KP duty after breakfast this week. No school today since it's Saturday."

As the two boys ate their hearty breakfast, several of the other boys finished theirs, cleared their plates and came over to the table to meet the "new guy." They were friendly and welcoming, but Hunter refused to let himself respond. He just kept eating without looking up.

When all of the boys had gone outside, letting the screen door bang shut behind them, Julius turned toward Hunter. "Hey, man, you don't have to take it out on them."

"Huh? Take out what on whom?" Hunter asked with some level of disdain.

"The guys. They were just trying to be friendly. Look, I know you're new and you probably feel a little scared…"

"I'm not…*ain't* scared of nobody."

"Yeah, I get it. But these guys are all struggling with their own demons. They aren't here to hurt you. And you'll find that they can actually help ya if you'll let them," responded Julius with a level of patience and understanding beyond his years.

As Betsy Fowler said during her brief orientation the day before, every boy on the ranch had chores. It took a lot of sweat to run a ranch and it was up to the boys to see that it got done. Chores were rotated on a weekly basis, changing each Saturday. Julius and Hunter were in charge of meal clean-up for the coming week. Looking at the pile of dirty dishes and greasy pots and pans awaiting them, Hunter quickly learned that there was a down side to the feast Mrs. Fowler prepared for each meal. Without saying a word, he rolled up his sleeves and set to work at the bubble-filled sink beside Julius.

They worked standing shoulder to shoulder, one boy with pale skin, reddish hair and bright, but sad, blue eyes, one boy taller, stronger, with dark skin, dark hair and determined but kind brown eyes. In the outer appearance, they could not have been more different. But on the inside...not so much. They worked in silence. Not because the jovial, friendly Julius wanted it that way but because he got tired of the grunts that served as responses to his queries. After several attempts to make conversation with his new cabin mate, he gave up and withdrew into his own thoughts, leaving Hunter to his.

Betsy Fowler bustled around the kitchen, making new messes as she prepared items for lunch. She hummed as she worked, all the while keeping a sympathetic eye on the new boy. He was hurting, that much she knew. The source of the pain was not evident to her but she knew she would find out eventually...she always did one way or another. "That looks great, boys," she said with a smile and a swat on Julius' backside with her dish towel.

Julius let out a fake bellow, turned and gave Mrs. Fowler a bear hug. She laughed with delight from within the circle of his strong arms. "Now, you boys go out and have some fun. I'll see you after lunch!" she said as she playfully pushed Julius away.

Hunter felt his face redden and he turned away in embarrassment. The overt displays of affection between Mrs. Fowler and the boys made him feel uncomfortable, though he couldn't have explained why.

The "fun" Betsy Fowler was referring to on this bright, hot Saturday, consisted of horseback riding games in the large arena. Boys were hooting and hollering as they took turns riding horses around the obstacle course that had been set up on the sandy surface of the arena. Hunter watched from the wooden bleachers that stood just outside the arena fence. The boards on the bleachers were sun bleached and splintered from years in the harsh desert climate.

Hunter watched with interest as the boys galloped their ponies and quarter horses around the arena, trying to carry eggs on spoons, grabbing rings from poles and racing around barrels as he had seen girls do in the county rodeo with his grandfather. After a while, Hunter's attention wandered over to the small corrals. He lifted his head up and peered over to the pens he had seen earlier in the morning looking for the little dun mustang. He jumped down from the bleachers and strolled over to the pens. Activity in a large round-pen into which several smaller pens opened caught his attention, and he wandered over to see what was going on.

A large dark-brown horse with a black mane and tail was running around the pen. In the center stood Smokey, the cowboy he met before breakfast. Smokey appeared to be ignoring the horse. He kept pivoting on the heels of his dusty boots so that his back was always to the horse. In his hand he held a rope that seemed to occupy his full attention. The horse, on the other hand, never took his eyes off Smokey as he cantered around the pen, hugging the fence.

Finally, tired of the game, the horse stopped, turned directly toward Smokey and let out a loud snort, his head and tail held high, his nostrils flared. Smokey appeared to ignore the horse as he walked calmly over to the gate and picked up a long white stick with a small, brightly colored flag on the end. He turned and faced the horse who was eyeing him suspiciously. The old cowboy stepped toward the horse and extended his arm, made much longer with the stick. The horse whirled away and ran the other direction. He made several laps around the pen before coming to a halt and turning to face Smokey.

Calmly, Smokey switched the stick to his other hand and extended his arm again. The horse tossed his head, whirled, and ran in the other direction around the perimeter of the pen. This time, he didn't run as many laps before coming to a halt and facing Smokey. Once again, Smokey, reflecting the serenity of a summer sunrise, switched the stick to the other hand and extended his arm.

Hunter watched in amazement as this was repeated over and over until Smokey could switch the stick and the horse reversed direction before he even came to a stop. It was obvious that Smokey had the horse's complete attention.

When the horse appeared to be getting tired, Smokey let the stick drop to his side and the horse stopped and turned toward him. However, there was no head tossing or snorting this time. Smokey took several slow steps toward the horse. The horse watched him, his ears pricked forward, until the cowboy was within a few feet. Then, he tossed his head, his forelock bouncing over his eyes, turned on his haunches and started running around the pen again. Hunter could feel a sense of disappointment and even frustration as he watched the horse run off. But Smokey's body language showed none of this. He simply walked quietly back to the center of the round pen and started repeating his stick pointing exercise.

Hunter took his attention off what Smokey was doing for a moment and looked over the small pens that were connected to the large round pen. Off to one side, he found the little dun mare standing over a pile of hay. But she wasn't eating. She was looking right at him with her moist, dark eyes.

For what seemed like several minutes, Hunter stared into the eyes of the little mare. Even after he wanted to look away, he couldn't seem to get himself to do it.

"Hunter."

The sound of his name being called broke what seemed to be a connection between the horse and the boy. Hunter looked toward Smokey.

"Hunter, watch carefully as I approach the horse. Notice how he keeps his eyes directly on me. If he moves away, then I'll put him back to work." Smokey moved toward the bay stallion. But this time, the horse didn't run off. He held his ground, his ears twitching every which way, his eyes locked on him. Ever so slowly, Smokey switched the stick and the rope into the same hand and reached out his other hand until he was touching the bay horse's forehead right between his eyes. Hunter could hear him cooing like a dove to the young stallion as he rubbed his head. Hunter was amazed but even more surprised to see Smokey turn and walk away.

The old cowboy walked through the gate and around the pen to stand beside Hunter. He rested his foot on the lower rail and his arms over the top. He looked at the stallion that had still not moved.

"We'll just let him think about that for a while," said Smokey with a smile.

"Why did you quit after all that?" said Hunter, squinting up at the cowboy, the bright sun having risen to its zenith for the day.

"Ah-h-h, boy. Good things take time. If you want his trust, you have to earn it. You can't rush it. I like to leave them on a good note. Leave them thinking about what just happened and that it was a good thing. He has to learn that I am not here to hurt him." Smokey turned his head and looked down at the boy. "Horses and people are a lot alike. It doesn't take much to destroy our trust but it takes a dang long time to earn it back."

Hunter could feel the muscles in his throat constricting and the backs of his eyes start to sting. He turned away and looked over at the mustang mare.

"What are you going to call her?" Hunter heard Smokey ask. He turned and looked at the cowboy, tilting his head and raising his eyebrows.

"She needs a name, you know. What are you going to call her?" Smokey repeated.

"Um, I don't know. Why do you want *me* to name her?"

"She picked you as her trainer so it's up to you to name her."

An idea popped into Hunter's head. "Mustang Sally."

Smokey nodded approvingly. "Let's go see how she likes it."

They walked over to her pen and leaned against the fence, the old man and the boy staring at the little dun mare with her light tan body and black mane and tail. She was very thin and burrs stuck in knotted clumps to her forelock, mane and tail. Her hooves were too long and chipped in several places. She wasn't much to look at that was for certain.

"She needs some tender loving care but with the right training she'll make a right fine horse, I'm sure of it," said Smokey, eyeing the little mare.

"How can you tell?"

"It's her eyes. I can always tell from the eyes." Smokey bent over and picked up a piece of straw. He stuck it between his teeth and used his tongue to shift it from side to side, all the while looking over the fence at the horse.

"Where did you get her?" asked Hunter.

"Adopted twelve of 'em from the BLM round-up."

Hunter was about to ask what that meant when Smokey continued. "The Bureau of Land

Management is in charge of all the wild mustang herds. When the herds get too big for the amount of forage on the plains, they round some of 'em up and put 'em up for adoption. I usually buy a few. Ain't nothin' better for trainin' a boy than a horse, I always say."

The two stood silently for a moment.

"So Mustang Sally, how do you like your name?" Smokey said kindly, as though the horse could understand every word. The mare brought her head up and nickered. Smokey let out a loud laugh. "Well, I'll be! She likes it! So, 'Mustang Sally' it is."

After dinner and kitchen clean-up, Hunter tucked an apple in his pocket and slipped out the back door of the lodge. The air had turned cool with the setting of the sun, and the first stars were starting to poke holes in the darkening sky. As he drew near the round pen and the little pens that surrounded it, he could hear the horses blowing and, occasionally, whinnying.

Hunter walked past several pens until he came to Sally's. He stepped up on the bottom rail with both feet and leaned over the top rail. "Hey Sally, I've got something for you," he whispered.

The mare lifted her head but didn't move.

He reached into his pocket. "Sally girl, looky here. Don't tell Mrs. Fowler, she might be mad, but I snuck a big juicy apple for ya." He stretched his hand outward but the mare still didn't move.

"Are you shy? Well, sure you are. I feel the same way. We've both been rounded up and put somewhere new and strange. Maybe we don't even belong here. You should be running free across the prairie. I should be..." he paused. He didn't quite know where he should be anymore. But he was reasonably sure it wasn't here in this rough country covered with dust and rocks and an occasional yucca, cactus and pinon pine. The mare looked at him with those penetrating eyes that he had seen and felt the first time he saw her. But she didn't make any attempt to move closer to him, even with the tempting apple being held out to her.

Hunter waited, not sure what to do at this point. "Well, I guess Smokey's right. It takes time to build the trust," Hunter finally said. He tossed the apple gently toward her. It landed a few feet in front of the little mare and rolled until it knocked one of her hooves. She slowly lowered her head and sniffed. Then, with one bite, the apple was cut in half. She chewed with her molars grinding from side to side, juice dribbling from her lips. Her eyelids drooped as she savored the sweet taste. She bent down and picked up the other half of the apple and repeated the process, enjoying it every bit as much.

CHAPTER 7

Building Trust

SUNDAYS WERE QUIET AND restful at Promise Ranch. Of course, the animals needed to be cared for and the boys needed their meals but chores were kept to a minimum. Church services were held in the large lodge. Afterward, the boys were encouraged to write letters home, read and relax. Several boys played one of the many board games that Mrs. Fowler set out on the tables. Other boys went back to their cabins to do homework or nap. Hunter didn't feel comfortable enough with the other boys to join in any of the games. Instead, he grabbed an apple from the kitchen and sliced it into quarters. Putting the apple in his pocket, he walked out to the horse pens.

Mrs. Fowler stepped out from the little room beside the kitchen that she called her "office," and watched him go out the door, her eyes focusing on the bulge in Hunter's pocket. She smiled, turned around and went back to her desk.

Hunter walked out to the arena, expecting to see Smokey working with one of the horses. Instead he saw the old cowboy sitting in a chair, his feet up on the rail of the fence with his hat pulled down over his eyes.

"What ya doin', Smokey?" Hunter asked.

Smokey pushed back the brim of his hat and squinted up at Hunter. "Ah, Hunter. Nice ta see ya. Ya caught me nappin' in the sun."

"I thought you'd be workin' one of the horses."

"Nah...not on Sunday. People and horses both deserve a day of rest as the Good Book calls it. And I intend to take full advantage of it," he concluded, pulling his hat back down over his brow and dropping his chin to his chest.

Hunter walked over to the horse pen to see the little mare. She was standing in the shade provided by the part of the pen that was covered to supply protection from the seemingly ever-present hot desert sun. Her head was hanging down as low as her knees, her eyes were closed, and her tail was lazily swishing at flies. Hunter climbed up, slid his feet through the fence and sat on the middle rail, his arms hanging over the top. He examined her closely, something he had started to do with the girls at his school. He'd blushed deeply whenever they noticed him staring at them. Here he was safe from that embarrassment at least.

He studied the mare's perfections and her imperfections. While she possessed the majestic beauty that all horses come by naturally, she was thin from lack of food and dirty from lack of grooming. He let his eyes memorize each angular curve of her body. Her coat though dull, was a beautiful sandy color. Her thick black mane was uneven and tangled with burrs. Her black tail was short and straggly. Her eyes...her eyes were beautiful but there was a deep mourning, reflecting a sadness in her soul, in those eyes.

He let out a long, low whistle. The mare lifted her head with a jerk, her ears pricked forward, now completely awake. But she didn't move from the shade of her shelter.

Instead, she just looked intently at him with those amazing eyes.

"Hey, girl, how do you like the name I picked for you...Mustang Sally? Do you like it? It's an old song. I'll bet you would like it if you heard it."

The mare continued to stare at him.

"Oh yeah. Look what I brought you." Hunter reached in his pocket and pulled out just one apple slice. He tossed it toward her. It landed barely outside the line of the shade. The mare slowly lowered her head and stepped forward. She snorted as she sniffed then used her lips to gently pick it up. She stood where she was and enjoyed the juicy morsel, her body now half way out of the shed.

Hunter let out another long, low whistle just like the previous one. The mare's ears twitched forward. "Here's another one," Hunter said, tossing the next apple slice a few more feet in front of her. Without hesitating, the mare walked forward again and picked up the apple.

The next toss was just a few feet in front of where Hunter sat on the fence rail, his arms and legs dangling into her pen. This time, the mare was far more tentative. "Come on, Mustang Sally. You know you want it."

Step by cautious step, the little mare moved closer and closer until she could stretch her neck forward and down over the apple. She stretched her top lip as far as it would go and pulled the delicious treat into her mouth. She jerked her head up and looked at Hunter while she ground the apple with her back molars.

Hunter sat still and quiet, not wanting to spook her. Slowly, he took the last apple slice from his pocket, held out his hand toward her and whistled his long and low signal. The mare stood stiffly, her eyes still on him, her ears still pricked forward. Hunter waited. After a few minutes, he whistled again. Sally's ears twitched forward and back but, other than that, she didn't move.

Hunter thought about what Smokey said about patience so he just kept waiting, occasionally puckering his lips and blowing his long, low whistle. Just as Hunter was about to give up and toss the apple on the ground, the mare took a step forward, just one step but it was toward him. His patience rewarded, he continued to hold out his hand and let out an occasional long and low whistle. The mare took another step. Hunter waited and whistled again. One more step and the mare was close enough to take the apple from his hand. Just then, several boys came around the corner of the barn, laughing and talking. The mare threw up her head, snorted and trotted away, head and tail held high, looking over her shoulder at the new arrivals. Discouraged, Hunter tossed the apple toward the center of the paddock and climbed down from the fence.

Kicking at the dirt with each step, the young teen stuffed his hands in his pockets and walked away. The chair that Smokey had been sleeping in was now empty.

As Hunter passed the barn he heard Smokey speak to him. "It takes time to build up trust."

Hunter stopped and peered into the dark opening. The bright sun shining in his eyes made it impossible to see inside so he walked over to the doorway. He stopped at the entrance to the barn and leaned against the rough wood that formed the frame. As his eyes adjusted to the shadowy dimness in the barn, he could see Smokey inside fiddling with a bridle.

"Were you talking to me?" asked Hunter.

"You'll make a mighty fine trainer for that little Mustang Sally of yours."

"I don't know anything about training a horse," responded Hunter.

Smokey immediately noticed the change in attitude but didn't comment on that. "Well, I 'spect you don't. That's why I'm here. I'll help you."

"Where do I start?"

"Trust. That's what I was sayin'. Ya gotta build up the trust. Ya break a horse with fear and domination. Ya train a horse with trust and patience."

"So are you saying you don't *break* a horse?"

"Yep, that's just what I'm sayin'. Just like people. Ya don't wanna break their spirit. Ya wanna mold it and shape it into somethin' beautiful. You are already starting to build up that trust with Mustang Sally. You nearly had her eating out of your hand. In another try or two, she will be. Just be patient." Smokey hung the bridle up on a peg and wiped his hands on his jeans. "So, boy, I'll see you tomorrow morning right after chores."

Hunter pressed his lips together and nodded his head. He turned and started walking toward his cabin. Facing the sun, he couldn't quite make out the face of the woman walking toward him, an odd shaped object hanging at her side, until she had nearly reached him. His eyes narrowed and squinted. Once he recognized who it was he stopped, folded his arms across his chest and said with a sneer, "What are you doing here?"

Melody winced, her chin trembling beneath red, puffy eyes. "I brought you your violin," she said as she extended her arm.

Hunter snorted then forced a laugh. "You came all the way out here to bring me that?"

"And I wanted to see what the ranch was like and...and...well I missed you," she added quickly. She looked down and her posture wilted like a dying flower.

"Well that was a big waste of time. You can leave and take that violin with you. I don't ever want to see it again." He wanted to say, "I don't ever want to see it or *you* again," but he just couldn't get himself to go that far.

Hunter turned his back on his mother. Seeing Smokey standing by the barn he felt a sudden tightness in his chest, his face flushed. But he set his jaw and said nothing.

Melody walked up behind him and slipped her free hand through his arm, "Hunter..."

His body tightened and he jerked his arm away. Hunter's mouth suddenly became very dry and he felt an intense thirst. His thoughts seemed to jump around in his head as he struggled with what to say and do. He really wasn't very good at this. He pushed away the feelings of love for his mother that were trying to take over. "I don't want to see you. I want you to leave," he said, refusing to look at her, his voice as stiff and tense as his body.

Melody dropped her head and slowly turned around. Hunter listened as her shuffling footsteps receded. He didn't allow himself to look back at her or at Smokey who, he knew, had watched the whole encounter.

It took quite a while for Hunter's pounding heart to calm and for his body to relax enough to move. He slowly turned, hoping his mother would be gone. Not seeing her, he let out a long breath, dropped his head and walked toward his cabin, kicking the dust as he moved.

As he stepped up on the porch, he stopped. He hoped his bunkmate was somewhere else so he could be alone. He wasn't liking himself very much right now and he doubted that he could be pleasant to anyone. He opened the screen door and heard its hinges squeak but no sounds came from inside. Relieved, he stepped into the cabin. He looked first at the fish swimming around the tank on Julius's dresser. The thought crossed his mind how odd it was that such a large boy would enjoy keeping those little fish. He realized that there was a lot he didn't know about his cabin mate. Right now he didn't really care.

He turned toward his side of the cabin and immediately noticed his violin case sitting on his bed. Hunter clenched his teeth. His hands formed two tight fists. Swinging his arms stiffly, he stomped over to the bed, intending to do...what? He didn't quite know. Grinding his teeth, he glared down at the black case. The young teen stood beside the bed, his fists pressed to his hips as sweat trickled down the sides of his face. His mind played out a vicious battle of emotions. One moment he was filled with anger, the next, sorrow. He followed that with resentment, then the overwhelming feeling of regret.

The struggling teen bent over and flipped up the two latches. Resting in its red velvet coffin, where he had intended to bury it, lay his violin. He felt his hands shake as he reached into the case and picked up the bow. Twisting the adjusting screw at the end of the bow, he tightened the horse hairs. With his left hand, he picked up the violin and cradled it between his chin and his left shoulder. With his right hand holding the bow, he confidently pulled the bow hairs across each string. G. D. A. E. All needed tuning.   As he had done hundreds of times, he turned the pegs to adjust the tightness of each string. Satisfied that the violin was in tune, he began to play. His fingers, rough from the work and dry, hot air, felt odd as they moved around and pressed on the strings. But the muscle memory he had developed through hours of practice guided him through Pachelbel's *Canon in D*. He closed his eyes and let the music carry him away. His body moved with the rhythm of the beautiful concerto. For six minutes the music filled the rustic cabin and embraced his heart. Tears flowed freely down his cheeks as he let the music carry him away. In the music he felt at home. He belonged here.

When the young virtuoso completed the piece, he lowered his violin and bowed from the waist toward his bed. A single pair of hands clapped, and he jerked around, startled to find that he was no longer alone. He quickly wiped the tears from his cheeks with his free hand as he blushed deeply. His cabin mate, Julius, was standing just inside the door grinning at him and clapping.

"Hey man, that was awesome. I really like Beethoven."

"It's Pachelbel," Hunter responded quietly as he quickly turned and put his violin back in the case.

"Pachelbel? I've never heard of him. Is he famous?"

"Yes, but he didn't write much."

"Too bad," said Julius with genuine admiration in his voice.

"I think so too," responded Hunter.

"So where did you learn to play like that?"

"Lots of lessons and even more practice," Hunter said with a smile, thinking back on the various teachers who had struggled to help him, especially Mrs. Wells.

"Well, Pachelbel, let's go get some grub," said Julius.

From then on, Hunter was no longer "Hunter" but "Pachelbel" to most everyone at Promise Ranch.

CHAPTER 8

The Horse Trainer

MORNINGS ON THE RANCH were the time for doing chores in an attempt to beat the heat of the desert sun. Julius and Hunter did their assignments in Betsy Fowler's orderly kitchen. As soon as they passed her inspection, they headed for the door.

"Hunter, aren't you forgetting something?" Hunter heard Mrs. Fowler say. He turned just in time to see an apple flying through the air toward him. With cat-like reflexes, he reached up and caught the apple. "You might want to cut it up," she added with a smile.

"Oh, yeah. Thanks," he said, feeling himself blush as he realized she was on to him. He stopped at the counter, found a knife and cut the apple into four sections.

Mrs. Fowler smiled then returned to stirring her pot of chili. "See you boys for lunch and afternoon classes," she called over her shoulder as the screen door banged shut.

Julius headed for the barn to tack up his favorite horse, the little paint that Hunter saw him riding on Saturday. He and two other boys were heading out to the far reaches of the ranch to check fences.

Hunter headed for the round pen where he knew he would find Smokey. He felt a surge of excitement run through him as he thought about learning to train a wild mustang.

He walked to the fence and climbed up. Smokey was in the center of the pen with the same horse he was working with on Saturday. This time, Smokey was not turned away from him but, instead, was moving around in a small circle with his right arm outstretched, holding the white stick that had a colored flag on the end. As he moved in a counter-clockwise circle, the horse moved as well, hugging the fence but keeping an ear cocked always toward him. As the horse cantered around the edge of the pen, Smokey calmly followed with his arm, as though he was pushing him from behind. He kept his body turned directly toward the horse's side.

After a few minutes, the horse slowed to a trot and turned his head toward Smokey. In response to this, Smokey switched the stick to the left hand and took a large step toward the horse's head. Immediately, the horse squealed, pinned his ears back, turned his body around and went the other way, picking up the canter again. Smokey nonchalantly followed with the stick pointing toward the horse's haunches and walked in a small clockwise circle as the horse cantered around the pen. Each time the horse neared Hunter, he swerved away, kicking up dust into the boy's face. But, all the while, the wild horse continued to keep his attention on Smokey. When the horse slowed to a trot, Smokey switched the stick to the right hand again and stepped toward the horse's head. The horse whirled around and headed back in a counter-clockwise direction but this time, he didn't squeal or pin back his ears and he went off in a trot instead of a canter.

After a few more changes in direction, the horse came to a stop and turned to face

Smokey. While softly humming a song, Smokey lowered his stick and his head and slowly walked back and forth in front of the horse. Hunter noticed that each time he changed direction he angled a little closer to the horse. The horse's ears pricked forward as he kept both eyes on the old cowboy, but he didn't move. When he was within a few feet of the horse, Smokey reached the stick slowly toward him and gently rubbed his face. The horse did not move. Smokey stepped forward another foot and casually extended his hand. The horse jerked his head up but still did not move. Smokey held his hand in place until the horse lowered his head. Gently, Smokey rubbed the horse's head right between his eyes, still humming his song.

Smokey turned and walked away from the horse and up to Hunter. "We'll let him think about that for a few minutes," the old cowboy said with a smile. "Hop down here. It's your turn now."

A wave of panic shot through Hunter. His muscles became tense and his heart began to race. "My turn? I don't know what to do."

"That's what I'm here for, boy," Smokey said with a smile.

Still uncertain about this idea, Hunter slowly, hesitantly, lowered himself into the round pen.

Smokey handed the white stick with the flag on the end to Hunter. "Don't be afraid," said the cowboy. "If you communicate fear to the horse, he will pick up on that and respond with fear toward you. Horses are herd animals. They are used to having a leader. You need to be that leader. If you communicate confidence, he will gladly follow your lead. A great thing about wild mustangs is that they naturally respect humans. Horses are not aggressive by nature. They are prey animals and their instinct is to protect themselves by running away. The round pen prevents him from running away so we can teach him to trust us and work with us." Then Smokey added with a chuckle, "just make sure he shows you his two eyes, not his two heels."

Trying to muster up enough courage to face a large and wild animal is a hard thing for anyone but for a teenage boy who has lost his way, it was especially challenging. Hunter wrapped his fingers so tightly around the training stick that his knuckles were white. Taking a deep breath, he looked toward the horse that was standing there looking back at him with far more confidence than the boy had within him.

Hunter took another deep breath, oblivious to the dust and the hot sun. "Okay, what do I do?"

The old cowboy patted him on the back then stood behind him holding onto both of his shoulders. He steered him to the center of the round pen and took hold of his arm that held the stick. "Now just keep your eyes on the horse, your body squarely facing his shoulder and flip the flag to get his legs moving. Keep your feet in place. You have to earn his respect. Whichever one of you moves his feet first, loses." Smokey controlled Hunter's arm and body from behind as a marionette would control a puppet. He made two kissing sounds and shook the boy's arm, making the flag bounce in the air.

Immediately, the horse's head jerked up and his eyes opened wide. One more kissing sound and he turned and started cantering away from Hunter's waving flag.

As the horse moved around the circular pen, Smokey guided Hunter's body, keeping him perpendicular to the horse, his arm and the stick following the mustang's haunches. Hunter felt himself smile as he kept his eyes glued to the moving animal. The horse's ears twitched back and forth, keeping track of the man and boy even when he didn't look at them. He was a beautiful horse, not large but quite muscular. Smokey's good feed had already added pounds to his frame and Hunter could see the strong muscles rippling under the shiny brown coat.

When the horse slowed down, Smokey switched Hunter's stick to the other hand and guided the boy forward a few steps toward the horse's front shoulder. The horse responded by turning toward them and trotting off in the other direction. "That's good that he is turning toward us. He ain't showin' us his heels. That's what we want."

Hunter immediately followed wherever Smokey directed him, feeling like partners in an intricate dance. The pattern was repeated several times. Each time the horse slowed down, Hunter switched hands and sent him off in the opposite direction. At last, the horse stopped and turned to face him, letting out a loud snort as he did so.

Suddenly, Hunter was aware that Smokey was no longer behind him moving his body around. A wave of panic flowed through him, and he looked around to find Smokey. Just as he did so, the mustang reared in the air and let out a loud whinny. He lowered himself back down to his front legs and began pawing the ground.

At that same moment, another loud whinny was heard splitting the dusty air. But this time, it came from one of the pens that was attached to the arena. The neigh came from the little dun mare. Her neck was stretched up as far as it would go so that her head was resting on the top rail of the fence. The young mustang turned to look at her and stopped pawing his hoof.

"Keep your eyes on the horse. Communicate that you're the boss," said Smokey, more loudly than he usually spoke.

Hunter jerked back around to face the horse. He could feel his heart pounding, and sweat running down his spine caused his shirt to stick to him. He took a deep breath and raised his chin, trying to project confidence.

"Good. Now get his feet moving again. Do just what you were doing before," Smokey said from where he sat on the round pen fence.

A bit timidly, Hunter raised his arm and pointed the stick toward the horse. At first, the mustang just stood there, as though trying to decide if this boy was serious and if he should bother moving.

"Show him that you mean it," said Smokey with a chuckle.

Hunter kept his eyes on the young stallion and shook the stick. The horse responded by raising his head a bit. Emboldened, Hunter clucked and shook the stick again, making the flag snap. He stomped his boot in the dust. The horse bolted to the side and started cantering around the pen again. Hunter looked briefly over at Smokey and smiled. The old cowboy gave him the "thumbs up" sign.

After several more laps around the pen, Hunter turned the horse around to the other direction. He let the horse canter, then trot, and then halt. As soon as the horse stopped, he turned and faced the boy, letting out another loud snort.

"Now, lower your stick and look away from the horse. This releases the pressure you've been putting on him and rewards him for giving you his two eyes," Smokey coached from the fence. Hunter did as he was told.

"Good, now move back and forth toward him, getting a little closer each time you turn around."

Just as he had seen Smokey do, Hunter moved very slowly, in a zig-zag pattern toward the horse. When he was close enough, he reached out the stick and gently rubbed the stallion between his eyes. Hunter felt a great wave of satisfaction and, yes, he could call it "pride" flow through him.

Just then, the clanging sound of the metal triangle that hung from the porch at the lodge rang out through the air. "That's it for today, cowboy. Time for lunch and afternoon school," said Smokey.

Remembering the apple slices in his pocket, Hunter said, "I'll be right there." He glanced over toward Mustang Sally's pen and noticed her looking through the fence boards, right at him. He went out the round pen's gate and walked over to her run. She pivoted and followed him with his eyes, head, and, finally, her whole body as he walked toward her. Climbing up on the fence, he leaned over the top rail and whistled low and soft. He held out his hand, showing her the apple. She didn't move but continued to look deep into his eyes.

"Come on over here, Sally. I have an apple for you." The mare twitched her ears and licked her lips but still didn't move. Hunter threw the apple half way across the pen. Sally lifted her head, swished her tail and stepped forward to retrieve the apple.

Once she had finished chewing, Hunter whistled again and held out another apple slice. "Come on Sally. This is for you. I won't hurt you. Just come over here and take the apple." He waited.

Mustang Sally blew air loudly out of her nostrils then took two steps forward. Deciding that was close enough, she stopped. Hunter rewarded her by tossing the apple half way between them. Again, she walked forward and grabbed the apple with her lips. When she looked up, she was only a few feet from Hunter and the boy was holding out another apple.

The little mare tossed her head and squealed. She whirled to one side, stopped and turned her head back to look at Hunter through the thick black forelock that had flopped over her eyes.

Hunter whistled long and low and kept holding out his hand. Hunter felt like he was in the middle of a dance where the two partners take turns leading. Right now, he was back in the lead.

Slowly Sally turned her body, pivoting her front legs around her hind until she was facing Hunter again. She took one step forward and stretched out her head and neck until she was nearly touching his fingertips. Lifting her top lip, she stretched just far enough to knock the apple slice out of Hunter's hand. She followed it to the ground and picked it up. Hunter waited.

When she lifted her head, Hunter had his last apple slice in his hand waiting for her. He whistled and she stepped forward. Slowly, yet calmly, she took it gently from his hand. The boy couldn't resist touching her face and stroking the soft black skin on her muzzle right between her nostrils. A flood of warmth ran through his body, and he felt as though it had been sent into him by the horse. He smiled broadly. "That's a girl, Sally. That's a girl."

CHAPTER 9

Dr. Collins

BY THE TIME HUNTER reached the lodge, all of the other boys and staff had already dished up their lunches.

"Hey, it's Pachelbel," shouted Julius from across the room. Julius then told everyone present about his talented, violin-playing cabin mate, not intending to ridicule but to praise. Hunter blushed and kept his head down as he walked toward the buffet table to grab a bowl of Betsy's chili.

As he was buttering a piece of cornbread, a small boy came up beside him. "Is that true? Do you really play the violin?"

Hunter looked down. The boy looking up at him with beseeching eyes was not more than twelve years old. He had blond hair and vibrant blue eyes. He looked like he should be a child model for a kid's clothing line, not living here at a ranch for troubled teens. But Hunter could tell by his timid demeanor that he was the type of boy who preferred to hide in the background. Approaching Hunter had obviously been hard for him. Hunter smiled to himself, thinking back on the old Hunter, the BT Hunter who had always been a front row kind of guy, a "Hermione Granger" student whose hand was always the first one up. Just the opposite of what he saw in this boy.

"Well, yeah. I try."

"Julius said you're really good."

"I used to work hard at it, but not anymore," answered Hunter as he grabbed two apples and started to walk away.

"I've always wanted to play the violin. Do you think you could teach me?"

Something about the obvious sincerity in the boy's voice made Hunter stop and turn his head. "You really want to learn?"

"Yeah, I really do."

Hunter stopped walking. "Have you ever tried playing a violin, or any instrument, before?"

The young boy shook his head.

"Why not?"

"Never had the chance."

"What makes you want to play one then?"

The boy dropped his head, and Hunter suddenly felt regret that he had asked. "No problem, you can tell me later. Okay?"

Without looking up, the boy nodded.

"Come to my cabin after dinner tonight and I will show it to you. I've never taught anyone how to play before so I don't know if I'll be a very good teacher..."

The boy lifted his face, revealing a broad, toothy smile. "Oh you will be! I just know it," said the boy, his bright blue eyes sparkling. "Thanks, Pachelbel!" The boy turned and nearly skipped across the large main room of the log lodge. Hunter watched him go and smiled to himself.

After lunch, the boys went to school. School for them meant sitting at one of the computers that lined the room and picking assignments from the program that was set up for each of them individually. Before Hunter could take a seat in front of the computer next to Julius, he heard his name being called. He turned to see a skinny, bearded man with wavy, graying hair walking toward him.

He stopped right in front of the boy and extended his hand. "Hi, Hunter, I'm Dr. Collins. I wanted to visit with you for a few minutes."

Hunter stood frozen in place.

"Hey, Pachelbel. Dr. Collins ain't gonna bite ya!" said Julius.

The man who had identified himself as Dr. Collins looked over at Julius and smiled warmly. "Thanks for the vote of confidence, Julius."

"No problem, Dr. C.," Julius said as he turned to face his computer screen.

"Well, Hunter, you heard it straight from the horse's mouth. I'm not going to bite you."

"I never thought you would," said Hunter quietly.

"No, I don't suppose you did. Come with me to my office and we'll get to know each other better."

Hunter followed the man across the big open room of the lodge toward a door on the far end. Dr. Collins led the way. When they reached the door, the doctor pulled out a key and unlocked it. This was the first locked door Hunter had yet seen at Promise Ranch.

"Come on in, my boy," said Dr. Collins, motioning into the room with one arm as he held the door open with the other.

Hunter walked in without responding. He wasn't sure if he liked this at all. Once inside the room, Hunter stopped and looked around. The room was warm and comfortable. A fireplace, similar to the one in the great room but much smaller, was directly in front of him. On either side, the walls were lined with bookshelves that reached to the ceiling. He drifted over to the shelves, feigning nonchalance, and glanced at the titles. He had once loved books, but that was the BT Hunter. The AT Hunter loathed them.

"You read these books?" Hunter asked over his shoulder while attempting to be uninterested.

"Oh yes," responded Dr. Collins enthusiastically as he stepped up beside the boy. "A book doesn't make it onto my shelf until I've read it. A book hasn't fulfilled its purpose until it has been read, I always say. Do you enjoy reading?"

"No way. Reading is for nerds," Hunter said with a snort.

"Well, I guess I am the ultimate nerd," responded Dr. Collins cheerfully. "Please sit down," the doctor said, pointing toward an over-stuffed leather chair with a cowboy print throw tossed over the arm. Hunter sat and watched Dr. Collins slide another chair up close to him...too close as far as Hunter was concerned. He decided right then that he liked the company of horses and even cowboys better than doctors.

"What kind of doctor are you?" said Hunter with almost a sneer on his face.

"I'm a psychiatrist."

"I don't need a psychiatrist."

"Great. We'll just be friends then," Dr. Collins said with a warm smile. *How many times have I had boys tell me* that *in the course of my career?* the middle-aged man seemed to be asking himself.

"I don't need friends, either," Hunter answered while twisting the corner of the throw.

"Everybody needs friends," Dr. Collins responded. His eyes reflected the ache in his heart that he felt for this boy.

"Not me. So called 'friends' just get you in trouble."

"Sometimes that's true. But not always. I guess it just depends upon the friends you choose."

Hunter frowned. He was eager to change the subject. Feeling very uncomfortable, he started drumming his fingers on the arms of the chair as he looked around the room. "Nice office you've got here."

"Thanks. It comes with the job. But I think Smokey has a better office, don't you?"

"What office?"

"I was referring to the barn with the horses. You like the horses, don't you?"

Hunter shrugged, "Yeah, I guess. They're all right."

"Oh, I think you like them better than just 'all right.'"

"Okay, so I like them."

"Good. We have something in common then. I like them too. So, are you getting enough to eat around here?"

"Yeah."

"That Mrs. Fowler sure knows her way around a kitchen, doesn't she?"

Hunter smiled in spite of himself. "My mom's a great cook too."

"Is she? Tell me about your mom."

Hunters face got red and he could feel the blood pumping in his ears. "I don't want to talk about her."

"Why not?"

"My mom's nothing but a stinking liar."

"What do you mean?"

"Every word she ever said was a lie!"

"*Every* word?" asked Dr. Collins, patiently.

"Well practically. She told me all my life what a great dad I had, how he was a war hero and saved hundreds of people's lives." Hunter blew out his breath, surprised at himself for letting so much slip out.

"And he wasn't?"

"No way! He's nothing more than a drug addict who sits around in jail!" Hunter could feel the tears behind his eyes, and he looked away so that Dr. Collins wouldn't see them. He felt angry at himself for opening up to this stranger.

Not fooled, Dr. Collins reached forward and empathetically touched Hunter's hand. Hunter quickly withdrew it. "I can see that you are holding in a lot of pain and anger," the counselor said.

"Well, yeah! Wouldn't you be?"

"Probably. But I don't know. I've never been in your position. But I do know one thing."

"Yeah? What's that?" said Hunter without taking his eyes off the picture of a cowboy praying that hung on the far wall.

"I know that you need to find a way to forgive her. You owe her and yourself that much."

"I don't see that I owe her anything. She's a liar," snapped Hunter, not liking this doctor or this conversation very much.

"In a way, that's true. But look deeper. Try to see into her heart. Why did she create a false image of your father?"

"Cause she didn't want to admit she had married a crook and a drug addict."

"Or?"

"Or what?"

"Or, perhaps, she wanted to give you a higher goal to be striving for."

CHAPTER 10

The Music Lesson

AFTER DINNER AND THE completion of the kitchen chores, Hunter walked slowly back to his cabin. He kept his head down as he walked, kicking at the dust and rocks that seemed to cover the entire ranch. He was regretting he told that little boy he would show him the violin. Come to think of it, he didn't even know his name. Not that that would matter. He still didn't want to see him. He was in no mood to speak to anyone, a fact that Julius could attest to after being forced to clean up the kitchen in silence.

As Hunter rounded the corner of the lodge, he looked toward his cabin and saw the little boy sitting on the edge of his porch, his short legs dangling over the edge of the gray weathered boards, not even reaching the ground. The boy saw him, jumped down and jogged toward him, his face beaming. Hunter was immediately filled with guilt for the negative thoughts he had been thinking. As rotten as he felt, it wouldn't kill him to spend a little time with this boy.

"Pachelbel! Pachelbel! I've been waiting for you," the boy said, his eyes sparkling with excitement.

"Hey, kid. By the way, what's your name?" responded Hunter, the boy's enthusiasm actually rubbing off on him.

"My name's Mark but everyone calls me 'Shorty.'"

"Do you like that name?"

The boy shrugged. "I don't mind. After all, I *am* the shortest one around here."

"And the youngest?" asked Hunter.

"Yeah, I guess so." The two boys walked side by side to Hunter's cabin.

Once inside the cabin, Hunter reached under his bed and pulled out the violin case. As he did so, he noticed a letter on his pillow. Shorty noticed it at the same time. "Hey, you got a letter!"

Hunter snatched it up and stuffed it in the top drawer of his dresser.

"Aren't you going to read it?"

"Yeah, maybe later."

"I sure would like to get a letter," said the boy.

"You don't get any letters?" Hunter was surprised.

"Naw. No one to write to me."

"What do you mean?"

"My mom's dead and I don't know where my dad is."

Sadness flooded through Hunter. Things really could be worse, like Dr. Collins had said at the end of their meeting. He hadn't seen how at the time. Hunter reached over and patted Mark on the shoulder. "I'm sorry, buddy."

"Ah, it's okay. I'm used to it by now." Obviously eager to change the subject, the young boy chirped, "So let's see your violin."

Hunter opened the case to the "oohs" and "ahhs" coming from Shorty. "Will you play something for me?" asked the boy with wide-eyed innocence.

Hunter put the violin to his shoulder, held it there with his chin and tuned each of the strings. Then he applied the bow and began playing *Meditations From Thais* by Massenet. The boy stood there in wonderment, listening to the music. His eyes were closed.

When he was done, Hunter lowered his violin and looked at the boy who was still standing there with his eyes closed and a smile on his face. Tears were wetting his eyelashes.

Quietly, Hunter said, "I asked you once before why you wanted to play the violin. You never told me."

Shorty brushed the tears from his cheeks and looked at the violin that Hunter was holding. Slowly and nearly inaudibly, he spoke. "The best years of my life were spent living with my grandmother. I lived with her for five years. She played the violin. Every night she would play for me when I went to bed." The boy looked into Hunter's eyes. "Do you know how great it is to be put to sleep with violin music?"

"Why aren't you living with her anymore?"

The boy looked down and shuffled his feet. "She got sick and put in a nursing home. They took me away from her because she couldn't take care of me anymore."

"Is that how you ended up here?"

"Well, after a couple of other stops that didn't work out so well," responded Shorty, still looking down at his feet.

"Do you like it here?"

At this, Shorty brightened. His head came up and he smiled as he said, "Oh yes! I love it here. Everyone is so nice. And I love the horses. Smokey lets me ride an awesome little horse named Magic." The boy paused and looked Hunter in the eyes. "Do *you* like it here?"

Hunter shrugged and turned away. "I don't know yet."

"You'll learn to like it here, I just know you will," said Shorty to his back.

Hunter didn't know how to respond so he did what he was getting good at...he changed the subject. He turned around and said, "So, let's start this violin lesson."

The lesson went quite well considering that it was Hunter's first attempt at teaching anyone. He found that it was much more difficult than he had ever anticipated. But Hunter did his best as he began showing Shorty how to play some simple melodies on the first two strings. As they were working, Julius poked his head in but quickly turned away. Instead, he sat outside on their porch and waited, listening to the squeaks from the strings.

After an hour, Hunter called it good for the day. Shorty thanked him profusely and headed for the door. Just as he was about to step out onto the porch, he turned and said, "Hey Pachelbel, don't forget to read your letter."

Hunter's face reddened, and he waved at the boy. Once the door shut behind Shorty, he went to his dresser, opened the top drawer and picked up the letter. The return address told him that it was from his mom. He wadded it up and threw it in the garbage can.

Julius stepped in the cabin just in time to see this. Yet, he said nothing about it. "Say, do we have a music studio going on here?" he asked cheerfully.

"Well, sort of. Shorty wants to learn how to play the violin."

"I was listening to the lesson. You'll be a great teacher for him."

Hunter snorted. "I don't know about that."

"No really. You are so patient. I'm not naturally very patient. That's a lesson the horses are trying to teach me."

Hunter ran his fingers through his hair. "Well, thanks. I guess I'll give it a try."

"I know Shorty will appreciate it. It was great seeing how he opened up with you."

Blushing, all Hunter could say was, "I'm going for a walk to see the horses." He picked the violin up from where it was sitting on his bed and lovingly placed it in its case.

"Do you want some company?"

"Naw. I won't be gone long, though." He grabbed the apple from where he had placed it on his dresser and went out the door. He didn't really know why he had turned down the offer for company. He couldn't help but like this kid with his cheerful attitude and the air of humility that surrounded him. Being alone wasn't always all that helpful. Maybe he just wanted to feel sorry for himself for a while longer.

The setting sun creates a sad kind of light as it says good-bye for the day. It seemed to be mimicking Hunter's mood as he walked toward Sally's pen. He tossed the apple up in the air, catching it as it came down. From down the row of pens, a small dun-colored head reached over the top rail, the eyes watching him.

As Hunter neared, the mustang mare let out a soft nicker. Hunter looked up and was immediately brought out of his melancholy mood. Clearly, Sally was calling to him. He responded with his long whistle. "Hi Sally, girl. You waiting for your evening treat?" he said softly as he approached her. This time, the mare did not move away, nor pin her ears, nor do any of the threatening movements that horses will do if they think you are in their space. She just stood there, calmly.

Hunter reached up his hand, holding out the entire apple like the witch in *Snow White*. Mustang Sally hesitated for just a moment before she took the apple out of his hand. She pulled her head back from over the fence and bit the apple in two, letting half fall to the ground at her feet. Hunter went up to the fence, folded his arms and rested his chin on them. He watched the mare chew happily on the apple.

From the darkness of the barn door, Smokey observed the entire exchange and smiled.

CHAPTER 11

Horse Training

THE NEXT MORNING, HUNTER arrived at the round pen to see Smokey working with the same bay mustang stallion that he had been working with the both times the boy had watched the trainer. It was remarkable how quickly the horse was learning to read Smokey's body language. Now all Smokey had to do was bend over and look at the horse's hindquarters and the horse would turn around. If he wanted the horse to speed up, all he did was point, cluck and slap the ground with his stick that now had a rope tied to the end instead of the flag. Soon, all he had to do was point and the horse responded by moving faster.

When the old cowboy saw Hunter standing at the fence, he turned and walked toward him. Now that the "pressure", as Smokey called it, was released, the stallion stopped and watched the old cowboy walk away.

Smokey stepped up to the fence, in front of Hunter and rested an arm and a leg on the rails. "Glad you got here. I have some more things I want to teach you."

Hunter nodded but said nothing.

"Horses are really two different animals in one big body. One of the animals reacts and one thinks. Now, take a wild mustang. Most of them have an over-developed reacting animal inside o' them. That's good because that's what keeps 'em alive. So, our job as trainers is to help that reacting animal get smaller and make the thinking one get bigger." Smokey turned to look at the stallion who was still watching him. "Look at him. You can almost see the thinking animal growing inside o' him caint ya?"

Hunter looked over at the stallion. His eyes were alert and his ears were pricked forward. He stood watching them while he licked his lips and, occasionally blew out a deep breath. Over-all, he seemed quite relaxed.

Smokey turned back toward Hunter. "Now that mare o' yours, she has an unusually large thinking animal already inside. I call it the 'thinking side of the brain.' Don't know where that came from but it's there without a doubt. She's a special one, she is."

Hunter felt himself smile. He liked hearing Sally referred to as his.

"Today I am going to help this horse become *de*sensitized to pressure. I have spent the last couple of days getting him to move to pressure. Now I want him to learn that he don't always have to run away from pressure."

Smokey lifted a coiled canvas rope off the fence post. He held it up for Hunter to see. "This here's a lunge line and I have a rope halter attached to the end. I'm gonna put this halter around his head."

Without further explanation, Smokey turned and walked up to the horse. With his hand that held the halter, he rubbed the horse's neck right behind the ears. The halter dangled down, bouncing against the horse's jaw bone and neck. The horse's eyes opened wide and his head came up but, other than that, he didn't move.

It happened so quickly Hunter didn't even see how he did it, but in a split second, Smokey had the halter over the horse's muzzle and tied over his ears. It happened so swiftly that the horse seemed not to have noticed, either.

Smokey stepped away from the horse and drew a circle around himself with the end of the stick. "This is my personal space. He doesn't get to come inside this circle unless I invite him," he said over his shoulder. Facing the horse, he tapped the stallion's chest and the horse immediately stepped back. He stopped tapping as soon as he moved. "That's the release of pressure. The release is the reward for doing the right thing."

Smokey started swinging the end of the long rope in his right hand. Startled, the horse jumped and started to run away. When he came to the end of the lunge line, the stallion felt the pressure of the halter and rope and started panicking, bouncing sideways. Smokey calmly followed, keeping the line tight but showing no signs of getting upset. As he moved along with the horse, he continued swinging the end of the lunge line with his right hand. Once the horse stopped moving away, Smokey continued to calmly swing the rope to his side, gradually getting it closer and closer to the horse until he was tossing it over his back, then his croup, then around his legs.

Hunter's eyes blinked several times then openly stared. He felt his skin tingling with amazement as he watched Smokey work. The horse actually allowed him to gently toss the rope all around him without moving.

After tossing the rope over the stallion's back and legs from both sides, Smokey let the rope drop. He stepped up to the horse's left side in front of the shoulder, talked calmly to him, patted him on the neck and released the rope halter. "That's enough for him to think about today," said Smokey as he turned away and walked out the gate.

Hunter left his perch on the fence and jogged up to Smokey. "Smokey, you said Sally was my horse. What did you mean?"

"Sometimes we pick the horse. Sometimes the horse picks us. If the horse has her heart set on a certain human, there ain't nothin' we can do about it. She's your horse, all right. She picked you," said Smokey as he gave Hunter a pat on the shoulder.

CHAPTER 12

Sally's Training Begins

THURSDAY MORNING WAS CLOUDY, unusual for a desert morning. The cooler temperatures were a welcome break from the intense sun that typically beat down upon the ranch.

The horses seemed to be appreciating it as much as the humans. Rather than standing around with heads drooping, they moved around their pens, whinnying and stomping, as though happy to be alive.

The whinnies awakened Hunter earlier than usual. He glanced over at Julius who was still sprawled across his bed, oblivious to the world. Hunter stretched his legs and arms out from under his quilt. He took a moment to watch the fish in Julius's tank swim back and forth while he thought about the lesson he gave Shorty the night before. Teaching was hard work, the teen decided.

Hunter's thoughts drifted to Sally. He thought he could hear her whinny above the rest. Hunter got up, dressed quickly and quietly left the cabin so as not to disturb Julius. He hurried down to the horse pens hoping to find Smokey.

As was expected, Smokey was with the horses, dishing out flakes of hay into each pen. "Hi Smokey," Hunter yelled over the commotion the horses were making. "Can I help you?"

"Sure thing! There's a little mare right over there that would sure like some hay, I reckon," Smokey said with a smile as he motioned with his head toward Sally's pen.

Hunter went to the bales of hay and pulled out a couple of flakes. "Is this enough?" he asked, holding up the hay.

"That'll be great. By the way, we're going to put Sally in the round pen today. So, after your chores are done, come back. I want you to do the training."

Hunter stopped in his tracks; he felt a lightness in his chest as feelings of excitement tempered by feelings of inadequacy mixed together within him. "Do you think I'm ready?"

Smokey laughed, "Now's as good a time as any, I'd say."

Hunter ate his breakfast quickly then impatiently waited around, wishing he could hurry the other boys. As soon as he noticed an empty plate in front of a boy, he rushed over.

"You done?"

"Yeah."

"I'll take your plate for you."

"Thanks, Pachelbel," was the surprised response.

Julius sensed the urgency. "So, what's the rush, Pachelbel?"

"Smokey wants me to start training Sally today."

"Ah-h-h," said Julius. "Well, let's get this done so you can get out there."

The two of them worked like a well-oiled machine, and the kitchen was cleaned up in record time. Even Mrs. Fowler was impressed. "Great job, boys," she said as she gave each of them a swat with her dish towel.

Julius laughed and aimed a swinging towel in her direction, missing on purpose.

"Don't you dare, you big lug," said Betsy with a giggle that sounded like a teenage girl.

Hunter headed for the kitchen door. "Oh Hunter, don't forget your apple," called out Betsy, sending one through the air.

"Good aim, Mrs. Fowler," said Hunter as he caught it. "Thanks!"

The moment he stepped out the kitchen door, Hunter noticed that the weather had changed. The clouds were lower and heavier. In the distance, he could hear the rumble of thunder. He jogged to the round pen, begging the weather to cooperate for just a little longer.

When he arrived, he found Smokey, hands on hips, staring at the western sky. "The Gods are up there bowling," he said with a chuckle. "Not sure how much time we'll have."

Hunter followed Smokey into the round pen. They opened the gate that opened into Sally's pen. The mare, feeling as frisky as all the other horses, trotted through the opening and into the paddock, head and tail high. She looked from side to side, whether checking out the scenery or showing off to the other horses, Hunter couldn't tell. But he did know that she looked beautiful and that made him smile.

"Now, boy, when you train a horse, just like everything you do in life, you begin with the end in mind. Where do you want to end up? Do you want a horse that trusts you or fears you? That is your slave or your partner? It all depends upon the choices you make right now."

Obvious to Hunter, the questions were rhetorical so he didn't respond. He just watched Sally trot around while he listened to Smokey share decades of wisdom gleaned from years of living with humans and horses.

Smokey set Hunter up in the center of the arena with the white stick in one hand. "Okay, just get her feet moving like I showed ya before."

Smokey walked back to the fence and climbed up onto the top rail. Chewing on a piece of straw, he watched his young protégée.

Hunter stood still for a while, just watching Sally and thinking about the things Smokey had said: begin with the end in mind. What did he want Sally to become? What did *he* want to become? This, like everything Smokey said, seemed to apply more to him than to horse training.

Okay, Hunter said to himself. *Let's get going.* He took a deep breath and reminded himself to breathe slowly. He let the air out gradually. He pointed in one direction, clucked his tongue and shook the stick, sending the flag on the end flapping. Sally's head turned toward him, and she started cantering around the circular pen. As he had done with the young stallion, when she slowed to a trot, he switched the stick to the other hand and stepped toward her head, causing her to turn and set off in a canter in the other direction. After repeating this a few times, Sally stopped and turned toward Hunter. She didn't snort the way the stallion had. She just stood and looked into his eyes, her ears pricked forward.

This time, Hunter felt much more confident. He lowered the stick and walked toward her with his hand outstretched. When he was no more than three feet away, he reached into his pocket and pulled out an apple slice. Holding it in his outstretched hand, he whistled softly. The mare stepped forward and took the apple from his hand.

Hunter turned around and smiled at Smokey. Before Smokey even had time to give him the thumbs-up sign, a bright flash of lightning and a loud clap of thunder shook the ground. Sally reared up and let out a loud squeal. Hunter stumbled backward and fell to the ground on his rear. Smokey jumped down from the fence and headed toward him but stopped suddenly. Before Smokey could even reach them, the mare lowered herself to the ground, right beside Hunter and curled her neck and head around him.

"Well, I'll be a monkey's uncle," Smokey whispered as he watched Hunter stroke her face.

The desert storm hit with a vengeance, and all the boys and staff ran for cover in the lodge where Betsy had sandwiches waiting for them. Julius listened to Hunter's story about Sally's response to the lightning. Once Hunter finished his story, the boy across the table who had been listening in, scoffed. "That's the biggest bunch of malarkey I ever heard!"

Julius stood and leaned his big, muscular body across the table and, with his dark face just three inches away from the other boy's, he said quietly but firmly, "Listen, boy, if

Pachelbel says it happened, it happened. Got that?"

The boy leaned back and raised both hands. "Hey, it's good by me, Julius. No problem, man."

"Good," said Julius as he lowered himself back into his seat.

After lunch, the boys started their schoolwork. Dr. Collins came out of his office and up to Hunter.

"Hunter, could you come spend some time with me in my office?" he said kindly.

Without saying a word, Hunter stood up and followed him across the large room to the counselor's office where the door was ajar, inviting them in.

Hunter made himself comfortable in the now familiar surroundings of Dr. Collins's office. He took a deep breath and waited for Dr. Collins to begin the conversation. He didn't have to wait long, a fact for which he was grateful.

"Hunter, what goals do you have for yourself?"

"Goals? Well, to be just like my father, of course," Hunter snapped.

"And what would that be...?" said Dr. Collins, twirling his pen between the fingers of one hand.

"A criminal. A drug dealer. A worthless bum."

Dr. Collins winced and cocked his head. "Those are your goals?" he asked, a mixture of skepticism and sorrow in his voice.

Hunter lifted his chin defiantly. "Yeah. All my life my mom told me to grow up to be just like my dad. Now I know what that is."

"Was that the kind of man she meant when she said that?"

Hunter let out a snort. "No. That's the big lie. She wanted me to be 'brave and strong and true,'" he said mocking his mother's voice.

"So did she really want you to be like your father?"

"Not my real father. Some fantasy father that doesn't exist."

"Can you separate the two...the real from the fantasy?"

"Can't do it. It's in my blood," Hunter responded arrogantly.

"Was it something in the blood that made your father do the things he did?"

Hunter looked up, his eyes staring blankly, deep in thought. He suddenly realized he didn't know his father at all. What had made his father do the things he did? What had motivated him? What had caused him to choose a life of drugs and crime? He had no idea. With no answer, he simply replied with a shrug.

Dr. Collins reached forward and patted Hunter's knee. "You may never know why he made the choices he made. But his choices are his. Your choices are your own. Are you brave enough to live the life you want to live?"

"Brave...." Hunter looked over Dr. C's head toward the picture of the cowboy praying and let the rest of the sentence trail off and float away.

In silence, Hunter returned to his computer in the main room. Dr. Collins's comments swirled around in his head. He tried to push them away. He attempted to focus on his school work. The tenth-grade curriculum Hunter had been assigned appeared on his screen and he looked at the list of subjects: math, science, history, language arts. Search as hard as he might, he didn't find one for horse training.

He smiled at himself. How his outlook had changed in just a week! Before coming to Promise Ranch, he had never, ever, given horses a second thought. Now, it seemed, he couldn't get Sally off his mind. Absentmindedly, he clicked on the math section and started to read the instructions for the Algebra II problem. But his thoughts kept drifting back to the morning and Sally...and then to Dr. Collins.

As he sat in front of the computer, the wind was blowing the rain against the windowpanes in front of him. He watched the water slide down the glass, distorting the view of the red bluffs that stood boldly behind the lodge. Hunter looked around him at the other boys, noticing how many of them were also looking out the windows. *It's funny how a good storm always gets everyone's attention*, he thought. He turned back to the computer screen and tried to focus. It wasn't long before he found himself looking back at the storm beating against the window as though trying to find a way to get in.

As he gazed through the moving water slithering down the glass, his thoughts went to the wadded up letter still sitting in the bottom of his trashcan. It was no longer alone. There were three more just like it on top...all unopened. His thoughts shifted to Sally and her desire to protect him from the storm. His eyes began to sting and the muscles in his throat constricted. He suddenly felt nauseated.

Hunter pushed back his chair. "I'll be back in a little bit," he said to Julius. "I don't feel so good." He ran out of the lodge. The wind and rain pummeled him as soon as he stepped out the door. At that moment, the clouds decided to send down pea-sized balls of hail, pelting him all over his body. No matter. He felt that, somehow, he deserved such treatment from Mother Nature.

Hunter jogged to his cabin, threw open the door, walked in and stopped. He stared at the garbage can. *Do I really want to do this?* he asked himself. *Why not? What can it hurt?*

Hunter soon learned that it can hurt a lot.

CHAPTER 13

Letters from Home

HUNTER PICKED THROUGH THE garbage until he found all four unopened and wadded up letters. Searching the postmarks, he found the one that had been on his pillow on Monday. The boy opened the envelope, pulled out the piece of stationary contained therein, smoothed it out and started reading:

My Dearest Hunter,

I am so sorry that I came to Promise Ranch without warning you that I was coming. It was one of those spur of the moment decisions that I made after spending the first night without you and not being able to sleep. I lay there in bed trying to imagine what you were doing and what the ranch looked like. Even though Grandpa said it was a great place and that he was sure you would like it, I just had to see it for myself.

It really is a beautiful place. Do you like it? I know you have never been away from home so I'm sure it is a little hard just being in a new place with new people. I remember when I was a little younger than you I went to Camp Fire Girls camp for a week. I cried every day, I was so homesick.

It sure is quiet around here without you. I miss you terribly but am hoping that you are having a great time. I pray for you every day.

Again, I'm sorry for coming unannounced. I love you so much,

Mom

The second and third letters were pretty much like the first with the addition of some event that had happened at work or in the town. It was the fourth letter that was different.

Dearest Hunter,

I haven't heard from you yet. I was hoping you would have written to me by now.

I have been going to a counselor to help me get through this hard time. I am struggling to understand where I went wrong and how I could have been a better mother to you. All I have ever wanted was to be the best mom you could possibly have.

I never, ever, intended to hurt you. When I told you those stories, for stories they were, about a fictional father, I just wanted you to have a role model to look up to. My counselor has helped me understand that I should have been honest with you about your father rather than try to hide him from you. I should have known you would find out about him someday so I should have helped you face the reality of his problems and helped you understand that those are his problems, not yours. I should have focused on the good role models you have around for you to pattern your life after.

I understand if you are still angry with me and never want to speak to me again but I pray every night that you will not react that way. I pray that you will find room in your heart to forgive me. I promise that I will never lie to you again, not at any time, not about anything. I will do whatever I can to repair the trust that has been destroyed.

Hunter, I love you more than life itself. You are my whole reason for living.

Please forgive me.

Your Grieving Mom

Hunter read the letter three times through. Then he lay on his stomach on his bed and buried his face in the pillow. His sobs shook the bed as the tears flowed freely.

CHAPTER 14

Julius' Story

WHEN HUNTER DIDN'T RETURN after an hour, Julius became concerned. He went to find Mrs. Fowler to tell her Hunter had left, saying he didn't feel well. Hunter's cabin mate told the ranch mother that he was going to go find him.

"Let me know if Hunter needs anything, won't you, Julius?" said Betsy, her mothering instincts on high alert.

"Sure thing, Mrs. Fowler."

Julius hurried out the door. The rain had eased up a bit but little rivers of water were making their way in front of the cabins. He splashed through them on his way to the cabin labeled "M Lazy C." He jumped up on the porch and opened the door. He stuck his head inside and saw Hunter's prostrate body face down on the bed. He quickly slipped his feet out of his muddy boots and stepped into the cabin. In just his stocking feet, he walked silently across the room up to Hunter's bed. He stood over him for a minute to make sure he was still breathing and noticed the rumpled letters around him. Relieved to see his shoulders moving slowly up and down, he gently shook Hunter's shoulder.

Hunter jerked up, startled at being awakened. He turned and squinted up at Julius, as though trying to figure out who he was. Finally awake enough to be aware of his surroundings, he collapsed back down on the bed but not before Julius noticed the dried tears on his cheeks.

"Sorry, man. I was just worried about you. You said you weren't feeling good."

"It's okay," Hunter mumbled into his pillow.

Julius backed away and sat down on his bed, still looking at Hunter. He took a deep breath to gather his courage then he said in a quiet voice, barely above a whisper, "You know man, I really like you. I'm glad you're my cabin mate. But we really don't know much about each other. Why don't we tell each other about ourselves? I'll start."

Over the next hour, Julius told Hunter about his life. He had been born in the bad part of Chicago where the police were afraid to go and gangs ruled the neighborhood. His mother had gotten pregnant as a teenager and never finished high school. They lived with his grandmother and paid their bills with welfare checks. His mom had been the third generation in her family to live from one welfare check to the next. He had never known his dad but he heard from an uncle that he was killed in a gang shoot-out.

When word of his father's death reached his mother, she sat him down and told him that she was not going to let that happen to him. She said that the cycle of poverty and violence she had lived with was going to end with the two of them. She packed up their few belongings that very day and walked him through the littered streets bordered by broken down cars. With head held high, she marched past the graffiti covered buildings with broken windows to the nearest bus station. His mother bought two tickets to Salt

Lake City, which was as far as her meager funds would take them.

They rode through the night, changing buses once in Denver. Julius slept and his mother worried. She had never known anything but the south side of Chicago and living on government assistance. Could she really support herself and her child?

Just as the sun came up over the Wasatch Mountains, the bus pulled into the terminal. With trepidation, the young mother stepped off the bus, gripping her young son's hand tightly, and looked around. What she saw shocked her. First, the air smelled so good. Second, the streets and buildings were clean and seemed to sparkle in the sun. The mountains to the east were enough to take your breath away as they rose sharply from the ground and seemed to guard the city with their mighty majesty. It was all so unlike anything she had ever seen, she thought they must have dropped into a fantasy world.

"Oh Julius, look at this," she said as they walked down the wide streets. This was soon followed by, "Oh Julius, look at that." Her excitement wasn't exactly contagious, however, and Julius pouted as he dragged his feet and complained of being hungry.

A passerby heard the child's whines and stopped them. "Can I help you?" the kind man said.

Immediately suspicious of all strangers, especially men, Julius's mother scooped him up into her arms and said, "No, we're fine."

Not taking that for an answer, the man said, "On the corner is a wonderful café. Let me take you there and get you some great home cooking."

"No really. We're fine," his mother insisted. But the man picked up her suitcase and gently guided her down the sidewalk. Perhaps it was this magical city or something about his kind manner, she didn't know, but for some reason his mother followed the man to the café.

Before breakfast was over, the man knew their entire story. "I think I can help you," he said.

"Oh, but you already have," smiled Julius's mother, truly grateful for his generosity.

The man smiled in acknowledgement of her gratitude but went on. "There's an old saying. 'Give a man a fish and you feed him for a day. Teach him to fish and you feed him for a lifetime.'"

Julius's mother looked at him questioningly.

"It means I want to help you be able to take care of yourself and your son. I know a wonderful family that recently lost their mother to cancer. The poor father is beside himself with grief. He has been left alone with six children to raise. He could use a housekeeper and nanny. He would pay you and give you and your son a lovely place to live."

"So, that is how we came to live with the Anderson Family in Salt Lake City," Julius said. "My mother believed in miracles from that day on."

"I can see why," interjected Hunter.

"Yeah. I guess so."

"So, how did you end up here?" asked Hunter.

"I guess some people don't appreciate miracles as much as others," said Julius with a sigh.

"What do you mean?" asked Hunter, glancing over at Julius.

"Well, you can take the kid out of the ghetto but you can't always get the ghetto out of the kid."

"You mean you got into trouble?"

"You can say that again. But Mr. Anderson refused to let me ruin my life. He sent me here with his own money. At first I thought he was just trying to get rid of me so I wouldn't be a bad influence on his kids. But Dr. C has helped me realize that perhaps he really cares about the choices I make with my life."

Julius stopped his narration, got up and walked over to his dresser. He leaned down and stared at his fish swimming around in the tank. After a while, he spoke again. "I love this fish tank. Mr. Anderson knew I wanted an aquarium so he gave it to me for Christmas. But when he gave it to me, he told me he didn't want me to limit my world the way the world is limited for these fish. It has taken me quite a while to understand what he was talking about."

While Julius talked about his life, Hunter lay on his back, his arms crossed under his head. He listened as he stared up at the ceiling, letting his eyes trace the patterns made by the knots in the wood just as he loved to do while staring at the stars in the sky on a moonless night.

Julius turned back, grabbed his pillow off his bed and chucked it at Hunter.

"Hey!" Hunter yelled cheerfully.

"Here I've spilled my guts all over the floor and you haven't said anything about your life," laughed Julius. "I'd say it's your turn."

Hunter rolled over on his side so that he was facing the wall. He breathed in deeply, smelling the dust in the air. His heart started pounding in his ears and he could feel the sweat forming on his forehead. He wasn't sure he was ready to talk about it but something about Julius's affable manner put him at ease and, surprising even himself, he started talking.

CHAPTER 15

The Trip to Town

SATURDAY ARRIVED, SIGNALING THE start of Hunter's second week at Promise Ranch. Other than Julius and Shorty, Hunter had not put in the effort necessary to get to know any of the other boys. He preferred the company of Smokey and the horses. His new weekly chore was cleaning the latrine - no one's favorite! But he and Julius got through it without too much complaining.

Once chores were completed, Julius made a gallant effort to convince Hunter to join the baseball game that was set up in the large sandy arena. Hunter declined. Instead, he walked over to the round pen and opened Sally's gate. She trotted into the pen from her run then immediately turned back and walked up to him. He began rubbing her face and neck. Cautiously, he moved toward her flanks. He lifted his hand and placed it gently against the mare's soft side. He felt a shiver go through her body and her muscles tensed. But, she didn't move.

Hunter felt the little mare's heart beating strongly and wondered if she could feel his, too. Soon the two hearts seemed to melt together and beat as one. Slowly, Hunter moved his hands around her barrel and down her shoulder. Equally slowly, both their hearts calmed.

"That's good, boy. She is learning to trust you, that's fer sure."

Hunter turned and saw Smokey leaning against the fence. The boy smiled and nodded, afraid to speak for fear that it would frighten her and the moment would be lost. When he left the mare's side, she followed him, walking a few feet behind, having learned the lesson of Hunter's private space, well.

Hunter walked up to the fence where Smokey still stood.

"Wanna ride into Rattlesnake Gulch with me?" Smokey asked. "I need to get some feed and salt licks. I think I'll even have enough left over for some ice cream."

"Rattlesnake Gulch?"

"Yeah, Rattlesnake Gulch is the closest town. It also happens to have the closest feed store."

Hunter shrugged his shoulders. "Sure, I guess." He hadn't been off the ranch since he had arrived nine days ago. On the drive here, he had been so consumed with anger and self-pity, he hadn't paid any attention to where they were going. He really had no idea where they were or how far away the nearest town might be. He walked to Sally's pen, opened the gate and led her into her enclosure, slipping her an apple once she was inside. He went out the other side of her pen, carefully latched the gate and walked across the yard to where Smokey was standing by an old truck.

They climbed into the pick-up and drove through the ranch on the long, bumpy, dirt road. Once they reached the highway, Smokey turned east and switched on the radio. The sounds of his favorite country western music filled the cab. Hunter listened to the songs about love going good and love gone bad. Then a song came on which amused him. He turned toward Smokey with a smile on his face. Raising his eyebrows he said, "Chewbacca, Chewbacca, Chewbacca, Spit?"

Smokey turned to him with a smile and a chuckle. Nodding his head he responded, "He's sayin' 'Chewtabacca,' Pachelbel. That there's real man music!"

Hunter snorted and rolled his eyes, but, secretly, he was enjoying the music with its real-life messages.

Smokey drove the pick-up along the road as it traveled east for several miles before making a long, sweeping turn to the north. As they drove along, the old cowboy, the wrinkles on his sun-baked face giving him a permanent smile, pointed out interesting rock formations. After several miles Smokey pointed to a dirt road that went off to the left. "Up there against that cliff is an old Indian settlement where they built caves in the wall of the cliff. They're called 'cliff dwellings' by the archeologists. Some are real tourist attractions like the ones in the Four Corners area. The ones up there are pretty much secret except to the locals and the scientists."

He turned and looked at Hunter, giving him a wink as though he was letting him in on the secret. Hunter shrugged his shoulders. He was curious but he certainly didn't want to show it. That was the BT Hunter.

"Sometime maybe I can take you there on horseback. It's quite interesting. Historians call the people that built the dwellings Anasazi Indians. They think they're the early ancestors of the Hopi and Zuni tribes that built communities all over Arizona and New Mexico, all along the Rio Grande. You should see the ladders they built to get up into the caves. The old ladders made from lodge pole pines and lashed together with rawhide are still there leaning up against the cliff. They carved their homes high off the ground for protection."

"What did they need protection from out here?" Hunter said, skepticism accentuated by his hand motions pointing out the bareness around them.

"Oh, I don't know. Wild animals, I suppose. Coyotes can be real trouble makers when they're hungry and in packs...kinda' like city boys runnin' in gangs," Smokey said by way of a joke. Hunter didn't think it was funny.

They rolled into the little town of Rattlesnake Gulch at the worst end of town.

Old houses in need of painting lined the road. On several houses, screen doors hung askew from one hinge. Clothing hung on bent and sagging aluminum clotheslines. Toddlers with drooping diapers played in grassless yards while mothers sat on porches and swatted at flies. Collarless dogs ran across the street in front of their truck.

As they reached the outer edges of what could be called the "business district," things became only slightly livelier. Much of the area was occupied by men and teens with too much time on their hands. Smokey pulled up in front of a large store. The sign across the front read "Rattlesnake Gulch Feed and Saddlery."

Smokey and Hunter climbed out of the truck and entered the store. To Hunter, the inside of the store looked like it was a hundred years old. The floor was made of well-worn planks of wood. The walls were covered with rough-hewn boards. It smelled of leather and sweet feed and sweat. On either side of the central aisle, heavy western saddles were displayed on stands, one particularly fancy one sitting on a life-sized statue of a black horse. The walls were lined with halters, bridles and ropes for leading and lassoing. Hunter could imagine some famous cowboy like Doc Holliday shopping here. They walked to the back of the store where a long counter separated them from several men in cowboy shirts and hats who were waiting to ring up their order on modern computers.

Smokey's order was large. "Ya got a lot o' head to feed out there, I hear," said the older man who was ringing up their order.

"Sure do. I adopted twelve mustangs from the BLM a little over a week ago. Skinny as rails they were, too. They bin eatin' like there's no tomorrow," Smokey added with a chuckle. "This boy's Hunter. He's gonna help me load up."

"That's good 'cause we're shorthanded today. Cain't seem to get any of the town boys to want to take a job. Ya might have seen 'em just hangin' around the street corners wastin' time and lookin' fer trouble."

Hunter picked up two bags of feed and headed out the door. Two doors down from the feed store, he saw some of the boys the man had been referring to. Three boys were standing in front of the small movie theater. Across the street was a badly weathered Greyhound Bus sign.

The town boys looked his way, casting quick glances first at him, then at the sign on the door of the truck: "Promise Ranch." One boy elbowed another and pointed toward him.

Hunter turned and walked to the back of the truck. Climbing up inside the bed, he busied himself rearranging the equipment to make room for the bags of feed. He could see out of the corner of his eye that the boys were walking toward him. He could hear them laughing and joking with one another.

As they approached the truck, one shouted, "Hey you!" Hunter looked up.

The one who had spoken appeared to be the ringleader. "You one of them criminals from out at the ranch?"

Hunter felt a surge of anger run through his body. He clenched his jaw and turned back to his work. He felt his muscles quiver as he moved a roll of wire up to the front of the truck bed. He didn't say a word.

"I'll bet you've got some skills we could use, don't ya!" All three boys laughed. They were now standing beside the door of the truck in a tight knot. Hunter continued to ignore them.

"Hey you! I'm talkin' to you. Didn't your mother teach you no manners?" said the boy as he pounded his fist in the palm of his hand. "Come on down here. Let's see what you're made of."

Hunter felt the anger start to build up inside of him, the kind of frenzy that is exciting and gets the adrenaline pumping. He had to admit, he kind of liked that feeling. It made him feel so alive. He stood up and turned toward the boys. Doubt started to level out the emotions. Three against one...not the best odds. He wasn't an experienced fighter. Did he really want to get into this? If not, was he really going to let these hoodlums goad him into a fight he didn't want? What had Dr. Collins said? "You're in charge of yourself. You don't have to let others make your choices for you." This fight was their choice, not his.

"Sorry, guys. Not interested," he said evenly and with as much calmness as he could muster. Trying to slow the pounding of his heart, he turned back to his work.

The boys erupted in laughter. "He ain't interested. Well ain't that nice. I don't recollect askin' if he was interested, do you?"

In a split second, the boys reached up and pulled him from the truck. One boy pinned his arms behind his back and the other two began punching and kicking him. Hunter attempted to struggle free. When that didn't work, he tried to use his feet to ward them off. He had never been in a fight before and didn't have great skills in this area. His feeble efforts were of little use.

The attack didn't last long before Hunter felt himself being shoved to the ground. For a moment, he just lay still, not sure what to do. Sunlight fell around him, warming his back. Dust filled his nostrils. He rolled over onto his back and squinted his eyes against the brightness of the sun. His mouth couldn't seem to open. He licked his lips and could taste blood. Suddenly, he was aware of yells and complaints from the boys. He turned his head to the left. All three boys were tied together with a lasso. At the other end of the rope was Smokey, a big smile on his face.

"I've seen newborn calves that were tougher than these three," he said as he gave the rope a tug, pulling all three boys over on top of each other. With arms pinned to their sides and feet intertwined, they fell hard.

Smokey walked up to the pile of boys and untied his rope. He wound it into a series of loops. "I don't want to waste a good rope on the likes o' you. Now, git!" he said, slapping his lariat against his leg.

The boys scrambled up and took off running down the street. Smokey went over to Hunter and helped him to his feet.

"I didn't fight them, Smokey."

"I know, boy. I seen what happened from the feed store." Smokey looked him over. "Well, coulda been worse, I 'spose. Still, Betsy Fowler ain't gonna be happy with me bringin' back damaged goods. Let's get that lip o' yers fixed up."

Hunter reached up and gingerly touched his rapidly swelling lip. Smokey led him across the street to the café. In the restroom, the cowboy dabbed Hunter's lip until he was satisfied that it was clean and done bleeding. "Ya know, boy," Smokey said with a twinkle in his eye, "one thing I've learned about life is that you never get used to getting a kick in the pants." The cowboy slapped the teen on the back. "So, how about a milkshake that you can drink through a straw?" he said with a smile.

CHAPTER 16

Training the Boy and the Horse

SUNDAY ARRIVED WITH ITS customary schedule. After church services and lunch, Hunter and Julius went back to their cabin.

"You gonna write your mom today?" asked Julius.

"I don't know," said Hunter, trying to avoid the question. In reality, he *did* know and he had no intention of writing to her. But he went through the motions of getting out a paper and pencil and plopping down on his bed. As soon as Julius had completed his letter and closed his eyes to take a Sunday afternoon nap Hunter tiptoed out of the cabin.

Hunter headed over to Sally's pen. *I'll bet if she had a mom, she'd be writing to her,* he thought with a smile. But joking, even to himself, didn't seem to make him feel any better. He kept thinking about the words his mom had written in her letter.

He picked up a rope that had been left on the ground. Hunter fingered the rope, feeling its rough ridges. "She lied to me," he said aloud, feeling his body tensing and heat flushing through his body as anger welled up inside of him again. For a moment it crossed his mind to throw the rope against the side of the barn but he sucked in a deep breath instead. Throwing a fit wasn't all that satisfying. The mustangs had taught him that.

As he looked around, he noticed Shorty sitting in the shade next to Smokey. Smokey was teaching the boy how to whittle. Little shavings had collected at their feet. Hunter walked over. "What ya doin'?" he asked.

Smokey and Shorty both looked up and smiled. "Smokey's teaching me how to carve. Look, I'm carving a horse," he said, holding up his work and revealing a shape that was a far cry from a horse.

"Um, that's really awesome, Shorty."

"Yeah, I know. Maybe someday I'll be a famous violin maker," he said, his eyes sparkling.

There was something remarkable about this kid.

"Do you want to learn?" asked Shorty, his big eyes examining Hunter.

"Naw. I'll just sit here and watch you."

Shorty immediately went into a narration that covered every second of the violin lessons they had had thus far. Hunter was amazed at the details that the young boy remembered. He made Hunter sound like the best teacher in the world. Smokey looked around Shorty, directly into Hunter's eyes and winked. "You really that good, Pachelbel?"

Hunter blushed, making his freckles disappear. "Well, I'm pretty good at playing, but I think Shorty's exaggerating a bit about my teaching. I've never taught anyone before."

"You're teaching Mustang Sally right well, I'd say. Just keep the end in mind like I always say. I think that applies to little boys and violins as much as to horses."

The next day Smokey helped Hunter with the training of Sally all morning, introducing her to the halter and desensitizing her to ropes and a saddle pad until they had her standing calmly while a saddle blanket sat on her back. Hunter was sad when the triangle clanged, signaling lunch time.

On the following day, Smokey had Hunter introduce Sally to a saddle. By this time, Sally was perfectly willing to wear a halter and be led around with a lead rope. Smokey started the process, slowly and calmly as usual. With Hunter at her head, the old cowboy walked around the mare with a saddle pad in his hand, swinging it at his side while he talked soothingly to her. Sally kept her eyes on Hunter, but her ears twitched back and forth, following Smokey's movement around her.

Smokey started rubbing the pad over her body. Hunter felt her tense up, but she kept her eyes on him and didn't move. Quietly, Smokey laid the pad on her back and moved away. Sally turned her head and neck and looked back at the pad as though remembering the strange feeling of having something on her back from the day before. She stood still.

"Now, lead her around, Pachelbel."

Hunter did as he was told. He turned and walked forward. At first, Sally didn't move but a gentle tug on the rope enticed her to follow him. Two complete circles around the round pen were followed with a bite of carrot and a rub on the forehead and neck.

Smokey got down from his perch on the fence and walked into the barn, returning a few minutes later with a western-style saddle hanging from one hand, straps and stirrups dragging in the dust. Sally watched him approach, her head raised and eyes wide open so that the whites of her eyes were visible. She turned back and nudged Hunter with her muzzle.

"It's okay, girl," he said as he rubbed her forehead. "We aren't going to hurt you. You know I will never hurt you."

As Smokey approached Sally's side, a swirl of wind sent up a cone of dust, filling Hunter's eyes with bits of sand. He closed his eyes and started rubbing them, just as Smokey swung the saddle onto Sally's back. The unfamiliar object on her back sent her jumping forward, right into Hunter and knocking him to the ground. The mare bolted and started running and bucking until the saddle and pad flew off and plopped to the ground with a thud.

Hunter, his eyes now clear, turned from his seated position and watched her go.

Once the saddle was off, Sally stopped and turned toward Hunter and Smokey. Her nostrils flared in and out as she snorted. Her head and tail were high. Slowly, she lowered her head and stepped toward the leather saddle that lay upside down in the dirt. She snorted with each step until she was standing over the saddle. She reached down and took a hold of one of the stirrups and lifted it, shaking it briskly. Then she dropped it back to the ground.

"Well, I guess she's telling us what she thinks of that," laughed Smokey as he helped Hunter back to his feet. "You all right, Pachelbel?"

"Yeah," said Hunter as he brushed off his jeans. "I just didn't see that comin'."

By the end of the morning, Sally was carrying the saddle around the arena without complaint as Hunter led her. As they walked, he talked to her quietly, stopping frequently to rub her face and neck. He was proud of the patience he had working with animals, a gift he didn't know he had until now.

At noon, Hunter went to the lodge, dished up his lunch and looked around to find Julius. His cabin mate was sitting at a far table, motioning for him to join him. The two boys were eating lunch while Hunter made a full report on his progress with Sally when Dr. Collins approached their table, leading a new boy.

"Julius and Hunter, this is Craig. He just arrived at Promise Ranch." Turning to Craig, Dr. Collins said, "Craig, I'd like you to meet Hunter and Julius. They are great guys and about your age."

Hunter looked up at the new boy standing slumped over beside Dr. Collins. The boy named Craig had a body made of ovals. Two tiny malevolent eyes were set deep on either side of a small nose, like buttons holding in his puffy cheeks. If there was any muscle, it would take a microscope to find it. The new boy looked away with a sneer and mumbled something like, "Yeah, sure," which everyone ignored.

"Sit down, and join us, Craig," said Julius in his typical cheerful fashion while motioning to the bench beside him.

Hunter looked over at his cabin mate, once again amazed at his outgoing, friendly personality. Julius had a talent for accepting everyone just like they were and not taking offense easily. He made a mental note to try to be more like him.

Craig plopped his overweight body down on the bench and sulked. "I don't want to be here and I don't want friends," he said with a snarl.

Julius looked at Hunter and winked. "Boy do we know how that feels, don't we, Pachelbel?"

"You don't have any idea how I feel," snapped Craig.

"Okay, whatever you say. But I'll bet you're hungry and we for sure know how that feels. Let's go get some grub." Julius pulled a resistant Craig up from the bench and led him to the table that was still stacked high with sandwiches.

With a little, no, a *lot* of food in his stomach, Craig was a bit more pleasant to be around. Only a *bit*, however.

"Oh, no," moaned Craig. "Here comes my stupid cabin mate." He ducked his head and looked the other way while Hunter and Julius turned to see who was coming. They both smiled in response to seeing Shorty weaving his way through the tables, his customary smile on his face.

"Hey guys! I see ya met my new cabin mate!"

Craig moaned and turned further away, if that was possible.

"Yeah we have. Sit down by us, Shorty," said Hunter, patting the bench to his side.

His eyes twinkling, Shorty joined the three older boys. "So, Craig, how do you like Promise Ranch?" he asked cheerfully.

Craig turned back to his food. A sound like a growl came from deep in his chest, but he didn't respond.

Hunter and Julius looked back and forth at the new cabin mates. Shorty just shrugged but kept smiling.

Hunter broke the awkward silence. "So, Shorty, you comin' for a lesson tonight?"

"You bet!"

The afternoon was spent doing school assignments. Hunter worked slowly, dreading returning to his cabin and seeing another letter from his mom. Mid-way through his schoolwork, Dr. Collins summoned him for a counseling session.

Hunter was surprised at his reaction. This time, he didn't resent spending time with Dr. Collins.

Dr. Collins seemed to notice his change of attitude. "You don't seem quite so angry today."

"I'm not."

"Can you tell me why not?"

"I like it here."

"Tell me what you like."

Hunter paused. There were so many things about Promise Ranch that he liked, but he didn't know what to share. "I like the desert...being away from the city. And, most of all, I like the horses."

Dr. Collins smiled and nodded. "I can agree with both of those. What about the people?"

Hunter looked over at the picture of the cowboy praying that hung over the fireplace. "Smokey is amazing," he said quietly.

"Yes, he is. How are you getting along with your cabin mate?"

"Oh fine. We get along really well. Julius is a great guy."

"He hasn't had the easiest life."

"I know. He told me."

"I'm glad he told you. It will help you understand him better, and, perhaps understand yourself better as well."

Hunter nodded. He didn't quite know how to respond to that last comment so he didn't say anything.

"By the way," Dr. Collins said, inserting himself into Hunter's thoughts. "You have a little boy that just idolizes you." Dr. Collins smiled broadly.

Hunter felt himself blush. "You mean Shorty...er...Mark?"

"That's exactly who I mean. He tells me all about his violin lessons."

"He tells everyone."

"I expect that he does. That's a good thing you're doing with that boy."

The rest of their conversation centered on Hunter's relationship with his mother. Hunter felt himself getting tense, and he showed this by twisting and untwisting the corner of the throw that decorated the arm of his big leather chair. For some reason that he didn't fully understand, he told Dr. Collins about the letters he had received.

"How did they make you feel," asked Dr. Collins gently.

"They just made me mad. I'm glad she's suffering. She deserves it."

"Have you written back to her?"

"No."

"Why not?"

"I don't know what to say for one thing. And I'm not ready to forgive her even though you told me I should."

Dr. Collins nodded. "I understand how hard it is to forgive someone. Especially someone you love so much. You know, Hunter, another thing I've learned about forgiveness is that it doesn't just happen all at once. It's a process. Sometimes it takes years."

Tears welled up in Hunter's eyes, and he brushed them away quickly. "Dr. Collins, sometimes I hurt so much."

Dr. Collins reached forward and patted the boy's knee. "I know. A broken heart causes real pain."

"How can I get this pain to go away?"

Dr. Collins wanted to take the boy in his arms and hold him. Instead he took one of Hunter's hands in his. "Hunter, the strongest people are those who have been to the depths of despair and climbed out. And I mean 'climbed.' Recovering from a broken heart is as slow a process as forgiveness. There will be days when you feel like you are making progress and then, the very next day, you will feel like you have slid backwards. Just like training a horse. Some days the horse seems to catch on to just what you are trying to teach and the next day it seems like they didn't learn anything. Try to be as patient with yourself as you are with your little mustang."

CHAPTER 17

The Bully

AFTER DINNER, SHORTY ARRIVED at Hunter's cabin with his customary enthusiasm for his lesson. However, this time, he was nearly a half an hour late. "Sorry for being late," he said with a grin. "Craig wanted me to help him unpack."

Hunter nodded and smiled. "No problem. I've got all the time in the world," he added with a chuckle. The lesson began like all of the previous ones: tuning each string, reviewing the musical scale and practicing the simple melody Shorty was learning. Hunter was pleased at the progress his first pupil was making. He felt the same way training Sally. He never realized how much fun teaching could be. It had never occurred to him before that his teachers, both at school and his violin teacher, Mrs. Wells, might actually *like* teaching!

His attention went back to his student and he corrected his position as well as his technique. He wanted the sound Shorty was creating to be rewarding. That was the best motivator to a beginning violin player.

Once the lesson was over, Julius came back in the cabin from his perch on the porch. Shorty piped up and in a manner of teasing said, "Don't you like my playing, Julius?"

Julius smiled. "It isn't that I don't like your beautiful violin music. It's just that I love watching the sunset and listening to the sounds of the desert. But, hey, great job, kid," he said as he gave Shorty a slap on the back.

"Thanks, Julius."

Hunter noticed how Shorty beamed at Julius's compliment. Julius had the ability to make everyone feel good about themselves. The teenager had already learned how to share a sincere compliment at just the right time. And the 'right time' for Julius was anytime he saw you. Hunter wished he could do that.

Hunter followed Shorty out the cabin door and headed for Sally's run. The mare was standing with her head over the top rail. He told himself she was waiting for him. Perhaps she was. This had become a nightly routine for the two of them. Hunter would come say good night and give her an apple or a carrot, whatever Betsy Fowler tossed his way.

Mustang Sally nickered as soon as she saw him approaching. Hunter climbed up on the fence, and she moved up beside him, anticipating a reward. "Hey, girl. You want a treat? Of course you do," he said, a big smile on his face and a warm feeling deep in his chest. He pulled an apple slice out of his pocket and held it in the palm of his hand, being careful to keep his thumb in and his finger's straight. The little mare quickly removed it with her lips and ground it with her molars, letting the juice drizzle out between her lips.

While Sally munched on the apple slices, Hunter examined her body. She had been at the ranch for nearly three weeks now and already she was looking much better. Her ribs and hip bones were no longer sticking out. The last two days, Hunter had been able to curry and brush her coat until it shone. With a comb and scissors, Hunter removed the burrs from her mane and tail. Much of her mane was lost removing the burrs, but Smokey assured him it would grow back. The boy looked down her thick, black legs and noticed that Sally's hooves were still too long and chipped. Hunter and the old cowboy had already worked on handling her feet, but they hadn't attempted using the rasp or nippers on them. Hunter realized they would need to do that soon. He started rubbing her face, noticing the way the hair on her forehead swirled in a circle. A gentle breeze came over the ridge, cooling off the air as the sky darkened and bringing the scent of the desert plants with it.

"That your horse?"

Hunter jumped, causing Sally to snort and back up a step. Hunter turned around. Craig was standing directly behind him, looking up with his head cocked to one side. A black t-shirt covered his large chest and belly, nearly camouflaging him in the gathering darkness.

"You startled me. I didn't hear you come up," responded Hunter.

"I said is that your horse?" said Craig, sounding more irritated than interested.

"Well, she belongs to the ranch but Smokey is letting me learn how to train her. He said she picked me."

Craig blew out a breath of air. "Horses can't pick people. They ain't that smart. You just have to show 'em who's boss."

"Well, that's not how Smokey does it. He says we *train* horses not *break* horses."

"Smokey's a fool then."

"No he's not. He's a great horseman. He really knows what he's doing."

"Don't sound like it to me," responded Craig. The boy turned and walked off, disappearing into the gathering darkness.

The next morning at breakfast, Craig came up to the table where Hunter and Julius were eating. He pulled out the bench and sat his large body down.

"No breakfast?" asked Julius, noticing Craig's empty hands.

"My boy's bringing it to me," he said with a smirk.

"Your boy? What do you mean?" asked Julius.

"You know, that little pipsqueak they make me bunk with."

At that moment, Shorty approached the table carrying a tray over-flowing with food. He set it down in front of Craig. "Hey! I told you I wanted ketchup on my eggs, you idiot. Now go get me some!"

Shorty cowered and stepped back a step. "Sorry, Craig. I'll go get some right now."

Julius stood up. "Just a minute, Shorty. You don't have to get ketchup for him. Craig can get his own ketchup if he wants it."

Craig glared at Julius. "Butt out o' this, black boy."

Julius ignored the racial slur and calmly addressed Shorty again. "Go get yourself some breakfast, Shorty, before it gets cold."

"I-I-I don't mind, Julius. Really I don't," Shorty stammered, taking another step back before turning and running back to get some ketchup.

Hunter could feel himself getting hot. He felt perspiration beading up on his forehead. He looked back and forth between Julius and Craig. The tension in the air was thick and ugly.

Julius slowly lowered himself back down onto the bench and stared at Craig, his dark eyes hard as steel.

Craig stared back with as much resolve. "I said to butt out o' this. It ain't none o' your business."

"It *is* my business. Shorty is my friend, and I will not sit by and watch him being bullied."

"You callin' me a bully?"

"If the shoe fits, wear it."

Craig stood up abruptly and picked up his tray. "Well, I ain't gonna sit here and get insulted!" He started to walk away. Then he turned. "You stay out o' my business or you'll regret it, black boy." Without waiting for Julius to respond, Craig stomped away and found another table.

Julius watched him go. Hunter watched Julius, his heart beating loudly in his ears. Julius seemed to be consciously trying to slow his breathing. Hunter watched him take his napkin and wipe the sweat from his forehead.

"You were amazing, Julius," said Hunter quietly.

His teeth clenched, Julius responded. "No. I just seen too many guys like him in my life. Just because they're big and fat, they think they can push everyone else around. They think everyone else will just stand by and let them. Well, I'm not going to."

"He's really not so brave, you know," whispered Hunter.

"Yeah, I know." Julius went back to eating his breakfast, stabbing his eggs with his fork and not looking up.

After breakfast, Julius and Hunter headed out of the lodge, passing Craig who still had a lot of food left to consume. Julius stopped beside him. "By the way, the name is 'Julius.'"

"Like I care," responded Craig without looking up from his copious meal.

Hunter felt chills run through his body and a sour taste in his mouth. *What's going to happen now?* he wondered, overcome with dread.

But Julius just shook his head in apparent disgust and walked out the door. Hunter followed, breathing a sigh of relief.

Hunter and Julius had the assignment to weed and harvest Betsy's vegetable garden for the week. They gathered their tools and started working. The sun was beating down on them even this early in the day, and they could feel the temperature rising quickly. No breeze was present to cool them off. Soon, they were taking off their shirts and soaking their undershirts in the hose to try to cool off. It was all in vain.

After they had been working nearly an hour, Hunter saw Craig and Shorty head for the chicken coop to complete their chore. Once they reached the chicken yard, Craig sat down on a bench beside the fence and Shorty opened the gate and went in. Hunter kept glancing over. As he watched, Shorty fed the chickens, gathered the eggs, and swept out the coop. All the while, Craig sat on the bench.

That night, Shorty was late for his violin lesson. When he finally arrived, Hunter noticed how quiet he was; the usual vivacious young boy seemed sullen, his hands clasped behind his back as he stared down at the floor of the cabin. Hunter ignored this and started the lesson, hoping that would cheer up the young boy.

When his lesson was over, Shorty stayed in Hunter and Julius's cabin, not saying much, just sitting on Hunter's bed.

"You gonna sit there all night, Shorty?" Hunter finally said.

"Oh, sorry. I guess you want me outta your hair."

"No. I don't mind if you want to stay. You have something on your mind you want to talk about?"

Julius, who had returned to the cabin after the lesson, turned away from his task of cleaning his fish tank and looked at both boys.

Shorty hesitated before responding. "Nah," he said as he slowly shook his head. He remained on the bed for a few more minutes as he twisted the patchwork quilt between his fingers. Without saying a word, he stood and walked out of the cabin.

Hunter and Julius looked at one another. "So, what was that all about?" asked Julius.

"I have no idea. He just seemed really strange."

"Maybe the little guy just isn't feeling good."

"Yeah, maybe that's all it is," responded Hunter as he stepped up to the screen door and watched Shorty walk toward his cabin.

The rest of the evening was spent discussing Sally's progress. "Smokey's the best horse trainer there is," Julius said. "You are learning from the master."

"He said I get to sit on her tomorrow."

"Really? I've gotta be there to see that!"

The sun continued to move south along the ridge of the western mountains, shortening the days as it went. Hunter wondered what winter in the desert would be like. His excitement over the promise of tomorrow made it difficult to sleep once the two teens turned out the lights.

After waiting for his brain to stop imagining himself riding Sally, he finally gave up on sleep. "You asleep, Julius?"

"I was trying," mumbled his roommate in a groggy voice that sounded like his mouth was full of marbles.

"Sorry, go back to sleep."

"I'm awake now. What do you want?"

"I was just thinking about Sally."

"That's a shock."

"Yeah, I guess I *have* developed kind of a one-track mind," Hunter said with a chuckle.

"Kind of!" said Julius as he let out a snort.

"Do you think she thinks about me at night?"

"Maybe."

"Do horses sleep?"

"Yeah. But Smokey once told me they only sleep for short snatches at a time, part of their survival instinct. They can even sleep standing up. I guess their knees and hocks can lock so they don't fall over."

"Really?"

"That's what Smokey said."

"Hum-m-m," Hunter responded as he stared toward the black night trying to encroach on their cabin through the window. "Do you think she remembers her training from today?"

"Remember what Smokey says about the two sides of the horse's brain...the thinking side and the reacting side?"

"Yeah."

"Well, our job is to help them develop more of the thinking side. Seems to me that the better we do that the more they remember."

"Makes sense," said Hunter.

"I've been watching some of your work with Sally. I think she already had a bigger than normal thinking side. So, I'll bet she'll remember it really well."

"Well," added Hunter as he rubbed the bruise on his hip from his hard landing that morning. "I can prove she still has a reacting side of the brain, too!"

"Smokey says they always will, no matter how well trained they are. Our job is to reduce it and get them to think first instead of react first."

Hunter rolled onto his back and folded his arms under his head. After a moment, he sat up and threw back the blankets. "I guess I'll go visit the bathroom." He slipped on his boots and quietly walked out of the cabin toward the latrine.

When he entered the always-lit bathhouse that all the boys shared, he heard someone in one of the stalls softly crying. Feeling a bit embarrassed about interrupting and not sure what to say if he was discovered, he silently stepped back outside. Curiosity prompted him to step around the corner of the building and wait to see who it was. The wait was longer than expected, and he shivered in the cold desert darkness. He wished he'd either gotten his job done or brought a coat. Just as he was about to give up and find a bush to hide behind, he heard the door open. Hunter immediately recognized Shorty. The young boy stepped out and slowly walked back to his cabin. Hunter watched him go but didn't say a word.

CHAPTER 18

Riding the Mustang

"YOU READY FOR THIS, today?" said Smokey as he gave Hunter a slap on the back.

Hunter made a face that reflected his doubts.

"Ah, you'll be fine, Pachelbel! It ain't too far to the ground!" shouted Julius from where he stood by Sally's pen. He followed this with a loud chortle.

"Thanks a lot, Julius," responded Hunter. Hunter entered Sally's pen and slipped the rope halter over her head, rewarding her obedience with a slice of apple provided by Mrs. Fowler. He turned and led her into the round pen where Smokey was waiting with the saddle pad and saddle.

The mare stood quietly with Hunter at her head as Smokey calmly placed the thick pad over her back. Hunter watched her eyes and ears for a response. Sally's ears twitched back and her eyes rolled a bit but she didn't move. When Smokey lifted the saddle and gently lowered it onto her back, Hunter felt her body tense and her muscles quiver. But her feet remained still.

"She's using her thinking side of the brain right well," said Smokey as he stroked her neck, shoulder and rump.

Smokey moved slowly back to her shoulder then bent down and reached under her belly, grasping the string girth that was hanging down from the other side of the saddle. Humming one of his favorite western songs, he brought the girth up toward the cinch and put the long leather strap through the ring at the end. The girth was just barely touching her belly. With the finesse born of years of experience, he looped the cinch around like a man putting on a necktie. Sally quivered again but did not move. "Okay, Pachelbel, let's take her for a walk, again. Nice and slow, just like you did yesterday."

Hunter followed instructions and walked Sally around and around the round pen until she seemed to forget that the saddle was even on her back. As he walked, he breathed in the pungent smell of manure, dust and sweat that seems to always hang heavily over horses, especially in the hot desert air. He forced himself not to think about the next step for fear he would communicate his nervousness to Sally. He wished his roommate would throw out some of his typical jokes to help him keep his mind off it a bit, but Julius and Smokey were both watching without saying a word.

"Okay, Pachelbel. She's doing great. Bring her over here," said Smokey at last.

Hunter turned toward the old cowboy and noticed that he had a sandbag dangling heavily from each hand. He brought Sally up to him and stopped, the mare stopping just behind him.

"Let's see how she does carrying a little more weight," said Smokey as he dropped one bag and carried the other to Sally's side. Slowly, he lifted one of the bags and set it on the saddle. Sally lifted her head and hollowed her back while letting out a loud snort.

"Easy girl," soothed Hunter as he shortened the lead rope and rubbed her face. Sally quivered and nudged Hunter's hand with her muzzle.

"Now take her for a walk again," said Smokey.

Hunter started walking and Sally followed him around the arena, stoically bearing her burden. The second sand bag was actually less of an issue, and she carried the added weight as though nothing had changed.

"Okay, cowboy. It's your turn," said Smokey as he placed a three-step mounting block that looked like a small plastic staircase a few feet from the fence. "Bring her up between the fence and the mounting block as though it is just another walk in the park...no big deal."

Sally followed Hunter between the steps and the fence with no more than a wary eye and a snort. She stopped as soon as Hunter did. Smokey removed the sand bags that had draped lifelessly across the saddle and took his place at Sally's head. "Step up there, boy, and lean your body across the saddle. Don't swing your leg over. Just lean against her and stay there."

Hunter trusted Smokey's skill as a horseman but not his own. The boy wasn't so sure that he was the right man for this job. Looking at Smokey with raised eyebrows and wide eyes, he silently pleaded for a reprieve from the assignment.

"Aye, go on. It'll be okay," said Smokey, swinging the end of the lead rope against Hunter's rump.

Taking a deep breath in an attempt to calm his nerves and slow his pounding heart, Hunter stepped up on the mounting block. He turned his body squarely toward the horse, grasped the horn of the western saddle with his left hand and leaned forward. Sally shifted to the side toward the fence and Hunter lost his balance. He jumped to the ground between the horse and the mounting block.

"Just try it again," coaxed Smokey.

Hunter slid the surprisingly light-weight steps closer to Sally and tried it again. This time, Sally stayed still though she did turn her head and look back at him.

"Now push down on the saddle with your chest, creating more weight." Step by step, Smokey guided Hunter through the whole process. Next he had him put his foot in the left stirrup and stand with all his weight on one foot. Finally he had him swing a leg over her back and sit gently down in the saddle.

Once in the saddle, Hunter felt himself unclench his teeth and actually smile. He held tightly to the horn with one hand, but with the other he reached forward and stroked the mare's neck.

Smokey turned and started leading the mare around the circle. Hunter let his hips relax and move in rhythm with the horse's strides. He sat up in the saddle and looked over at Julius who had been silently watching the whole process. To his surprise, Julius was not alone. It seemed that every boy on the ranch was peering over the fence.

CHAPTER 19

More Bullying

THAT EVENING, ALL THE talk around the dining tables was about Hunter and Sally. This was the first time any of the boys had actually been asked to be the first to back a wild horse. This made Hunter a bit of a superstar and the boy liked the feeling. He found himself laughing and joking for the first time since his arrival at Promise Ranch. He enjoyed talking to some of the boys he had never spoken to before. Julius remained at his side, being the commentator and sifting through questions.

Just as dessert was set out, Hunter noticed Shorty enter the dining hall. A sharp pang of guilt at having failed to notice the little boy's absence before now swept through him. "Hey,

Shorty, grab some dinner and come join us," Hunter shouted over the joviality.

Shorty looked up, and his dour expression changed instantly to a broad smile. He nodded and waved as he went over to the buffet table. As he was walking back toward Hunter's table, he passed by Craig, seated with his back to Hunter. The large boy stuck out his long leg and big foot just in time to send Shorty sprawling forward. The young boy landed hard on his front, his face planted deeply in the spaghetti he had dished up on his plate.

Julius saw the entire thing and jumped to his feet with Hunter close behind. As Hunter helped Shorty, Julius confronted Craig.

"Hey you big thug, what do you think yer doin'?"

Craig looked around, apparently to see if any staff had noticed. Seeing none nearby, Craig stood up and faced Julius. Putting his nose up to Julius's he sneered, "What did you call me, black boy?"

"I called you a thug," replied Julius, not in the least intimidated. "But I can think of a lot worse names to call you. Like 'bully,' for instance."

"Bully?" sneered Craig. "I ain't no bully. I can't help it if the kid can't walk without falling down."

"You tripped him and I saw every bit of it. And if I ever see you picking on him again I'll…"

"You'll what, black boy? You don't scare me."

Hunter stepped up beside his friend. "I saw it, too, Craig. This better stop or you'll have both of us to deal with."

Craig lifted his hands in the air, palms toward Hunter and Julius. "Oh-h-h-h, I'm scared!" He rolled his eyes and snorted with derision.

By this time, the confrontation had caught the attention of Dr. Collins.

The counselor stepped between the three boys, two of whom were much larger and taller than he, and pushed them apart. "Hey guys. What's the problem?"

Craig immediately put on a façade of politeness. "Oh, nothing Dr. Collins. We were just having a little conversation, right guys?"

"Not exactly, Craig," said Julius, still glaring at him.

"Well let's find a way to discuss our differences without threatening one another," said the counselor. Turning, Dr. Collins noticed that Hunter had returned to helping Shorty get cleaned up. "Why, Shorty, what happened to you?"

After glancing quickly over at Craig, Shorty responded, "Oh, nothing, Dr. C. I just tripped and fell."

"I'm sorry. Go get yourself some more dinner."

"I don't think I'm hungry anymore," whispered Shorty.

Hunter felt sweat gliding down the center of his back and his hands started to feel clammy. He glared angrily at Craig who had turned away and returned to his large helping of spaghetti. As surreptitiously as a cat, Hunter stepped up behind him and pushed his face into the plate.

Several boys seated nearby burst into raucous laughter. Craig wiped his face and glared at Hunter. "You'll regret you did that," he sneered between clenched teeth.

CHAPTER 20

Craig's Revenge

TRAINING SALLY BECAME THE center of Hunter's attention. He hung on every word that flowed freely from Smokey's mouth. As soon as morning chores and breakfast were complete, he went to Sally's run, put the rope halter over her head and began grooming her. By the time Smokey arrived, he had the saddle on.

The bridle with a soft bit for her tender mouth was introduced as slowly as everything else along the way. Within a week, Hunter was riding Sally around the arena, stopping and starting and turning circles with ease.

The afternoon school assignments were such a bother as far as Hunter was concerned.

But as Betsy Fowler always reminded the boys, "no work, no play." Sally was considered play to her, of course not to Smokey.

A week after the incident with Craig in the dining hall, Hunter and Julius returned to their cabin to get cleaned up for dinner. They were talking excitedly about Sally's progress when they stepped into the little cabin. Both boys stopped suddenly. Lying on the braided rug that covered the wood floor between their beds was the shattered remains of Julius's fish tank. A wet circle covered half the rug. Scattered around the darkened spot were all Julius's little fish, lying dead on their sides. Julius dropped to his knees and cried.

While Julius grieved, Hunter bent down and began gently picking up the slippery, little bodies. He found a small box that he lined with tissue and reverently placed the fish into it. He covered them with yet another piece of tissue then put the lid on the box.

He walked over to Julius and patted him on the back. "Shall we go find a place to bury them?" he whispered.

Julius wiped his tear-streaked cheeks with his sleeve, nodded his head and stood up. Without saying a word, he followed Hunter to the barn. Hunter handed Julius the homemade fish coffin. The distraught boy stood, head bowed, while Hunter found a shovel and dug a hole in the soft dirt at the back of the barn where he was sure it would not be disturbed.

"It's ready," he said when the hole was deep enough.

Without saying a word, Julius walked over, bent down and gently laid the box in the hole. Hunter watched and wondered if he should say a prayer. Do people pray at funerals for fish? He had no idea. He had never been to a fish funeral before. Julius solved the problem.

"Thanks for being such good friends," he said as he whispered each fish's name. "Swim free and swim far."

Hunter covered the box with the dirt.

Both boys had their suspicions about how this had happened. After all, fish tanks don't just walk off a dresser by themselves. But, without any proof, they decided to, at least for the time being, keep their suspicions to themselves.

They walked silently across the yard to the dining hall, stepped up on the porch, the sound of their boots on the wood the only thing breaking the silence between them. The screen door squeaked on its hinges and the delicious aroma of Betsy's dinner wafted out. The boys stepped into the large room together.

"Hey Julius! We're having fish for dinner!" Craig shouted from the end of one table. Two boys sitting with him broke into boisterous laughter.

Hunter looked at Julius, unsure of what his reaction would be. He saw his friend's jaw clench, the muscles twitching. The veins on his forehead bulged beneath his dark brown skin. Little beads of sweat popped up and clung precariously to the tight, coarse curls that covered his head. But he stared straight ahead and kept walking. Hunter was impressed with his cabin mate's self-control. He wondered if he would ever be able to develop the same sort of internal strength that he was learning to admire so much in Julius.

That night, Hunter left the cabin to pay Sally a late night visit and bring her an apple. It was a dark, moonless night. It appeared to Hunter that the desert nights seemed to be getting colder and colder with each passing day. The smell of dying sage filled the air. A few uprooted sagebrush bounced against his legs, being rolled along by the gentle breeze.

Even before he rounded the corner of the last cabin, he heard the high-pitched screams of a horse. He started running. In the darkness, he saw a horse running wildly around the round pen. He knew immediately that it was Sally.

In the center of the arena, a dark figure was shouting while cracking a long whip over her back and legs. Hunter placed his hands on the top rail of the fence and, in one adrenaline-fueled leap, cleared the fence. He landed in the soft dirt of the arena and started running. Like a football player going in for the tackle, he lowered his head and rammed into the back of the person wielding the whip, driving him to the ground. He rolled the boy over. Craig lay in the dirt beneath him.

"What do you think you're doing?" shouted Hunter.

Craig started laughing. "What's the big deal? I'm just training your stupid horse."

With one hand on Craig's throat Hunter raised his right fist and was about to use it to rearrange Craig's nose when he heard a shout.

"Hey, what's goin' on out there?"

Craig took advantage of the distraction to roll out from under Hunter. He stood quickly.

Even in the darkness, Craig would be able to see the anger in Hunter's eyes. Putting on the role of the polite young man that he had learned to play around adults, Craig responded. "Oh good evening, Mr. Smokey, sir. Don't be concerned. Nothing is wrong. Sally got out of her pen and we were just trying to get her back in."

Smokey opened the gate and walked into the arena. Hunter remained on the ground panting. Craig stood and smirked at him though it was barely visible in the darkness. Sally stood still and watched from the side of the arena, her sides heaving, her nostrils flaring in and out.

"Smokey, I found Craig chasing and whipping Sally," he choked out, barely able to contain the fury he felt inside.

Smokey turned to Craig. "Young man, this is my territory. You step in it, you answer to me. Now git out before I use that whip on you. And don't come back until I invite you."

Craig gave a snort. "Yes sir, Smokey sir." He turned and walked toward the gate.

"Craig," Smokey called to his back.

Craig stopped but didn't turn around. "Yes, sir?" he responded with an inflection in his voice that indicated he felt he was superior to this old cowboy and resented having to kowtow to the likes of him.

"I'll see you at 6 a.m. for stall cleaning," Smokey said through clenched teeth.

"I thought I was to stay out of your territory."

"Unless yer invited and yer now invited."

The next night, Shorty came for his lesson. He was late again, an occurrence that had become commonplace. The young boy walked into the cabin. Hunter greeted him enthusiastically and extended the violin toward him. Shorty didn't reach for the instrument as would be typical. Instead, he kept his right hand behind his back.

Hunter looked at him as he cocked his head to one side quizzically. "What's the matter, Shorty? Why are you hiding your hand?"

Shorty didn't respond. He just stood there with his head down.

"Let me see your hand."

Shorty still didn't move.

Hunter set the violin down on the bed and walked up to the boy. He gently moved Shorty's arm around to the front. What he saw made him gasp. Shorty's hand was black and blue and swollen to twice its normal size.

"What happened to you?" Hunter said.

At this, Shorty started crying.

"Julius!" Hunter called. "Come in here!"

The alarm that rang in Hunter's voice brought Julius out of his chair on the porch and back into the cabin.

The two boys examined Shorty's hand. "I think it's broken," said Julius.

"I do too," responded Hunter. Looking at the weeping boy Hunter repeated his earlier inquiry. "How did this happen?"

Shorty sniffed and stuttered. "I can't tell you."

"Craig," said both older boys at once.

"What are we going to do?" asked Hunter, his wide eyes beseeching Julius.

"We are going to Mrs. Fowler," replied Julius as he helped Shorty to his feet and gently guided him out the door.

If you want a solution to a problem, Mrs. Fowler is the one to go to. Never the type of person to let grass grow under her feet, she always seemed to know just what to do.

The boys walked to the back door of the lodge. They opened the screen door and rapped on the rough wooden door that marked the entrance to Mrs. Fowler's private apartment. After several knocks, Mrs. Fowler appeared in a thin, well-worn bathrobe and pink spongy curlers in her hair. The boys had never seen anyone so beautiful in their lives. Mrs. Fowler ushered them in and took over from that moment on.

Shorty was taken to the nearest hospital, seventy miles away. His hand was set in a temporary cast until the swelling went down and brought back to Mrs. Fowler's apartment where he was made comfortable and treated like a king.

Craig was picked up by his parents the next day. Hunter and Julius watched him go with smiles on their faces.

CHAPTER 21

Training the Boy

"NOTHNG AND NO ONE on the face of God's green earth is perfect, Hunter," Smokey said, still looking down at Sally's hoof as he artfully pulled the rasp over it. He set the hoof down and examined his work. Pressing his hands on his aching back, he stood upright. "Ain't no one perfect. Everybody makes mistakes. It's what they do to fix the mistakes that counts. Sounds to me like you've got some fixin' to do, son."

It had been two months since Hunter had arrived at Promise Ranch. Yet, he still had not found the strength or courage, or whatever it took, to write to his mother. She had contacted Mrs. Fowler who had conferred with Smokey.

Now Smokey was approaching Hunter in the only way he knew—straight on.

Hunter no longer felt the desire to argue or fight back. Instead he just listened as he watched Smokey work on Sally's feet. Her hooves were so long and uneven when she had been adopted that the correction had taken several sessions with the rasp and nippers once Sally trusted them enough to let them handle her feet.

The last line echoed in Hunter's head: "You've got some fixin' to do, son."

What does he mean, I've *got some fixin' to do?* he asked himself. He noticed that Smokey had stopped talking and working. He was usually doing one or the other, or both.

Hunter looked up. Smokey was standing with one hand on the mare's rump, staring at him. "What ya thinkin' Pachelbel?"

Hunter took a deep breath. "I'm wondering why you said *I've* got some fixin' to do. *I* didn't do anything."

"That's the problem ain't it? You haven't done anything."

"What does that mean?"

"What's Dr. C been talkin' to you about?"

"He says I need to forgive my mother."

"Have you?"

Hunter paused and pursed his lips. He felt his body tense and his hands clench into fists. "No," he said in a whisper.

"Then I say again, you got some fixin' to do," said Smokey. The old cowboy let his last statement hang in the air as he bent down and picked up Mustang Sally's hind hoof.

Smokey, Hunter and on occasion one or two other boys enjoyed going for long rides across the desert. They worked their way around prickly pear cactus and rocky outcroppings and down arroyos as they skirted the mountains to the north of the ranch. Most of the land had been leased from the BLM or the National Forest service for grazing of cattle. It took a lot of land to feed the small herd of cattle that Smokey looked after.

On this day Smokey and Hunter were alone and their ride was for the purpose of finding that herd and checking on their condition. Winter was on its way and Smokey needed to figure out if it would be necessary to bring the cattle into the ranch to feed. He also needed to take a head count to make sure he hadn't lost any cattle in the month since he had checked on them. The two cowboys, for that is what Hunter now considered himself, set off to the northwest. A cool desert wind was blowing, carrying with it the scent of sage. The sun was low in the southeastern sky, having just risen for the day, warming their backs.

Hunter rubbed Sally's neck as she followed dutifully behind Kit, Smokey's favorite trail horse. Kit wasn't a Quarter Horse or Mustang like the rest of the herd. He was a tall, lanky Thoroughbred that Smokey rescued off the race track twenty years before. He had kept Kit with him ever since as the old cowboy moved from ranch to ranch before finally settling at Promise Ranch a few years earlier. Kit was patient with the new mare that wanted to stay on his heels for protection, having mentored many young horses and wild Mustangs over the years.

"Where're we headed, Smokey?" asked Hunter as he melted into the saddle, moving his hips with the rocking motion of his horse.

"Well, we're goin' ta check their favorite spots. If I guess right, we'll be back for Mrs. Fowler's lunch. If I don't, we'll be sleepin' under the stars tonight."

Hunter wasn't sure which of the choices presented by Smokey he wanted to see happen.

They continued west, following an arroyo that wound its way toward the mountains. The footing was soft and sandy, and they were able to lope along, enjoying the ride. Sally's canter stride was short and a bit choppy, but Hunter, as inexperienced as he was, was none the wiser. He just bounced along enjoying the day and the desert views, unencumbered by trees. The arroyo took them to the entrance of a canyon that cut into the mountains. Smokey slowed Kit to a walk. Sally followed Kit's lead and slowed down as well. The two horses and riders worked their way up the canyon, climbing up rocky ridges until they reached the top where a wide plateau spread out to the north.

It was on this plateau that Smokey expected to find the little herd. But the dry summer had left the land void of any fodder; as unparticular as cattle are, there was still nothing they would eat.

Smokey shrugged his shoulders as they stood looking around. "Well, it looks like we won't be back at the ranch for lunch."

Hunter sat atop Sally, rubbing her neck. "Is this the type of place Sally lived in when she was in the wild?"

"Yep, I 'speck so. Or someplace pretty much like it."

"Why was she rounded up?"

"Too many horses, not enough food. If the herds get too big, they'll all suffer and many will die. The BLM manages the herds by making sure they don't get too big. On dry years like this one, they have to round some of 'em up and put 'em up for adoption. Mustangs make mighty fine horses once you get into their hearts."

Sally let out a snort, turned her head and neck, and nuzzled the toe of Hunter's boot.

"And that mare sure has let you into her heart," added Smokey quietly.

The two men, one young, one old, rode across the dry land to where a windmill pumped water into a large, round water trough. A tiny trickle of water coming from a pipe, kept the trough full. The numerous hoof prints in the soft dirt around the trough indicated that the herd had been there recently.

As Sally dipped her head and drank deeply from the cool water, Hunter looked around at the magnificent scenery that surrounded them. The sun was still on their backs as it slid silently across the southern half of the sky. The desert wind was stronger on the top of the plateau but the smell of sage was gone. Hawks let out an occasional cry as they floated on the wind currents above them, in their constant search for food. To the north, the mountains stood tall and imposing, void of snow. While he couldn't see any cattle, there were signs of them all around. He remembered that their dried manure had been used by the pioneers who settled the west as fuel for fires when they crossed the plains.

Once the horses had their fill of water, Smokey turned them to the west. The plateau slopped gently down in this direction, and they rode to the edge where a trail wound its way back and forth as it descended to the valley floor. Halfway down, they heard the mournful bellowing of a calf.

"That don't sound good," Smokey mumbled.

"What do you mean?" asked Hunter.

"Sounds like someone's in trouble."

Once on the flat, the two picked up a lope and headed in the direction from which the sound was coming. On the back side of a rocky outcropping, Sally stopped, jerked her head up and let out a loud snort. On the ground in front of them, was the problem. Tangled in the remains of an old barbed-wire fence, a cow lay on her side, exhausted from having struggled for who knew how long and the loss of blood from the deep cuts the wire had caused. Her calf stood beside her, the source of the sorrowful sounds they had heard.

Smokey tossed his reins to Hunter and leapt from his saddle. He walked quietly up to the cow, talking softly in an effort to comfort her. The last thing he wanted was for her to start struggling and cause more damage. He knelt down on the ground beside her and began examining the situation. It wasn't good. The poor cow had apparently become entangled in an old barbed wire fence that was partially buried under the sandy soil. She had fallen and in her struggle to get up had badly cut her hind legs and hindquarters. The muscles were ripped so severely, she would never walk again. Now she lay on her side, her breathing labored, her eyes half shut. Her little calf stood beside her, bellowing.

Hunter watched in silence as Smokey returned to his horse and unbuckled his saddlebag. The old cowboy pulled out a small revolver and walked back to the cow. Hunter turned his head and squeezed his eyes shut, waiting for the sound he knew was coming.

"Hunter, take the horses to the other side of the rocks," said Smokey. Hunter opened his eyes and looked over at the old cowboy. Smokey was standing in front of the cow, his gun pointed at her head.

Immediately, Hunter turned Sally around and nudged her into a trot, holding tightly to Kit's reins. The two horses and the boy disappeared around the large boulder.

BANG!

Startled, Sally jumped forward, nearly unseating Hunter. His grip tightened around the saddle horn and he brought her to a stop. Within a few minutes, Smokey appeared from around the back side of the rock, carrying the little calf.

"This little feller's goin' ta need some tender lovin' care back at the ranch," he said as he put a rope gently around his neck. "Now I'm goin' ta make sure that don't happen to any more o' my cows." He replaced the revolver and removed some wire cutters from his saddle bag.

"Can I help?" asked Hunter.

"Sure," said Smokey over his shoulder as he trudged through the sandy soil back to where the cow lay lifeless.

"Why'd ya have ta kill her?" asked Hunter, softly, sensing Smokey's sorrow.

"She'd never walk again. I didn't want her eaten alive by the coyot's or mountain lions. Better this way."

"You gonna just leave her here?" Hunter asked as he dismounted and tied Sally, Kit and the calf to the branch of a dead tree.

"Sure hate to. Good meat on her. But we're too far away and I didn't bring anything to carry it home in. Seems a waste, don't it?"

"Yeah, it kinda does."

"Well, look at it this way. We made some big cat's day," Smokey said with a chuckle. "Actually, those cats much prefer to catch their own dinners. They like the challenge of the chase."

"I kind of like it served hot on a plate," said Hunter, smiling.

Smokey slapped him on the back. "Yeah. Me, too."

Smokey untangled the barbed wire, cutting it where he needed to, and rolled it into a tight ball. Hunter pulled up the remaining pieces from where they had been covered by wind-blown sand and rolled them up as well. They searched the area for more pieces of fencing until they were sure they had cleaned everything up. No more cattle would find their end here...at least not from the actions of man.

The old cowboy pushed his hat back and wiped his forehead with his neckerchief. Letting out a long breath, he looked toward the west where the sun was painting the clouds a bright pink as it marched toward the western mountains. "Looks like we better bed down here for the night. I don't like the idea of tryin' to find my way home in the dark with a green horse and a greenhorn."

"Who's a greenhorn?"

"Well, ya ain't what I call 'experienced,'" added Smokey with a snort.

Hunter smiled. He knew Smokey was just teasing him. Then again, he really was pretty new to all this outdoor stuff, and a night under the stars sounded like a great adventure.

Hunter took the horses a short distance off and let them drink from a tiny stream that had managed to survive the dry summer. Smokey built a fire and cooked some of the meat from the cow. Hunter felt embarrassed to be eating the calf's mother right in front of him so he turned away. "Do you think he knows we're eating his mom?" he asked.

"Naw. Cattle ain't that smart. He's just glad I've got some mush to give him," Smokey said as he let the calf lick some moistened feed off his fingers.

Once the sun set, the desert night descended like a cold, black specter. Hunter shivered and wrapped his bedroll tightly around him. The horses snorted and stomped and the little calf snuggled against his leg. He moved closer to the fire for warmth, dragging the little calf with him and wrapping him in his blanket. The image of snuggling beneath an afghan with his mother flashed across his mind, and he pushed it away.

"I want to tell you a story, Hunter," said Smokey as he gazed at the crackling fire. In the darkness, Hunter looked toward the cowboy but didn't say anything.

Speaking slowly, Smokey continued. "Once there was a young boy who was being raised on a ranch up in Montana. It was a hard life and his chores kept him busy from sunrise to sunset. He fed the livestock, herded the cattle, cleaned and repaired tack, mended fences—on and on. The chores were never ending. One night, he decided he'd had enough. He took off his boots and cowboy hat and put on some regular old tennis shoes and a baseball cap. He crawled out his bedroom window onto the roof of the porch and jumped across to the big tree limb that hung close by. As quick as a cat, he climbed down the tree and ran away."

Hunter sat up and pulled his knees up to his chin. He looked through the dancing flames at Smokey's face, painted gold by the firelight. He reached over and stroked the little calf. *I know where this is going*, he thought. Yet he sat silently, letting Smokey tell his story.

"He thought life away from the ranch would be wonderful...freedom...no chores...no one to boss him around and tell him what to do. But life wasn't what he thought it would be for a runaway. He roamed around the highways and little towns feeling lonely and lost. He begged in the streets for measly bits of food and a shelter over his head. After a while, he wished he could return home to the ranch, but he didn't know if his family would take him back."

The cowboy reached forward and stirred the fire with a stick. For a few minutes, Smokey sat silently, poking at the fire. A coyote howled from somewhere in the darkness. An owl hooted from a nearby tree. Finally Hunter spoke up. "What happened to him?"

"Well, one day, after months of wandering around and suffering, he made up his mind to go back to that Montana ranch. As he walked beneath the familiar log beams that formed the entry to the ranch, he saw his father galloping toward him on a horse. Before the horse could even come to a stop, his father leapt off its back and ran up to him, taking him in an embrace that nearly popped his eyes out." Smokey chuckled at the image his story had conjured up in his mind.

Poking a stick once again into the embers, Smokey pulled one small piece away from the warmth of the flames. The bright orange glow soon faded and the little piece of charcoal became black as it cooled. Hunter watched and waited. Smokey pushed the little piece back into the base of the flames and, before long, it was once again glowing merrily.

Hunter looked over at Smokey and discovered that the old cowboy was looking back at him.

Hunter returned his gaze to the little piece of charcoal that now glowed brightly nestled in next to the logs and burning embers.

Smokey snored loudly in his bedroll. Hunter smiled to himself as he thought that the snoring alone would keep them safe from any desert predators. He folded his arms under his head and gazed up at the stars. He thought back to his science lessons. These twinkling lights had traveled for millions of years through the vacuum of space to sparkle for him. He didn't know if that made him feel important or completely insignificant.

Hunter discovered that sleeping outside wasn't all it was cracked up to be. Once the fascination with the stars wore off, he found that attempting to sleep on the ground on a desert winter night was nothing if not uncomfortable. His whole body was cold and hurt from lying on the hard ground. Add to that the strange sounds that kept reaching his ears. Some sounds, like the munching and sneezing of the horses, were fine. But the hooting of the owls and the cracking of branches, from what he knew not, kept him awake all night. From the continuous sound of snoring coming from the other side of the fire, Hunter knew that none of this bothered Smokey.

Nights can be very long sometimes. And they can be very hard to endure when your mind reruns unhappy scenes over and over. Hunter shook his head to dislodge the memories that kept plaguing him. Nothing worked. Slowly, so as not to disturb the little calf sleeping beside him under his blanket, Hunter got up and walked over to Sally.

"Hey, girl," he said as he rubbed her face. She responded with a soft nicker. "I know you've spent lots of nights like this. How come you're not sleeping?" He ran his fingers through her uneven mane. The course hair of her mane stood up in sections where he had cut the burrs out of it. Other places, the hair fell halfway down her neck. It wasn't very pretty. He made a mental note to take some scissors and even it up a bit when they got back to the ranch. "Oh, yeah. Now I remember. Julius told me you don't sleep for very long at a stretch. Always on the lookout, eh?"

Hunter threw his arms around her neck and pressed his face against the warm skin. He breathed in deeply of the sweet horse smell, a smell he had come to love. "Are you happy at the ranch?" he whispered. "Or do you wish you were still wild and running free?" In his mind, Hunter started counting the advantages and disadvantages Sally had living at the ranch. Without realizing how it happened, he transferred his count to himself. He wasn't really free either. He had been sent to Promise Ranch against his will, probably just like Mustang Sally. Yet, he realized he actually liked it there. He had learned a lot about the great outdoors, horses and, most importantly, himself. Maybe Sally felt the same way.

Hunter turned and looked through the darkness to where the soft light from the fire lit the bump in his blanket that was the orphaned calf. His heart hurt for the little guy.

Surely he is missing his mother, he thought. Had his mother kept him warm at night? Had his mother tried to protect him? His throat constricted and the backs of his eyes stung as he thought of his own mother. He thought of the pleading in her letters, the pain that it reflected. The pain that he had caused. As if a bright light suddenly illuminated his heart, he realized the part he had played in this whole mess. He was filled with remorse for what he had done to her. That was surely as bad as what she had done. His aim had been to hurt. Her intention was not anything so sinister. Her mistakes were made out of love, misguided though they were. His mistakes were made out of anger and a desire for revenge. All of a sudden, Hunter thought of the piece of coal, black and cold due to its separation from the warmth of the rest of the burning embers.

At last, he understood. Hunter's heart burst, which is quite the opposite of breaking. His heart seemed to become so large that it filled his body with its warmth. The joy that surged through him like an electric current seemed impossible to contain. He couldn't wait for the sun to rise so they could return to Promise Ranch. He had something he needed to do. Something that was long overdue. He needed to write to his mother.

CHAPTER 22

Repenting

THE SUN SEEMED TO rise slowly, painting the eastern sky in shades of pale blue and pink like a baby's nursery. The two cowboys had very little left to eat, just some trail mix and beef jerky. And they were getting dangerously low on water. Smokey and Hunter still had a long day ahead of them. Hunter took the horses and the calf over to the little spring to drink their fill. It might have to last them for the rest of the day, he didn't know for sure.

"Let's find those cattle and get back to the ranch. I sure could use some of Mrs. Fowler's cookin' right about now," said Smokey as he saddled up Kit.

Hunter couldn't agree more. Yet, his mind was ignoring his stomach for the most part. He was busy composing a letter to his mother in his head.

They rode slowly to the west, pulling the calf along behind them. By noon, they finally found the little herd, grazing peacefully in a low valley that still had some fodder.

Smokey made his count of the herd and discovered, to his pleasure, that the cow he had shot the day before was the only one missing. Several calves were bouncing around beside their mothers. Their little orphan let out a long bellow and was answered by others in the herd. With Smokey assured that the herd was fine, they turned and rode slowly back to the ranch.

By the time they reached the ranch house, the sun had set and the half-moon was floating behind soft ribbons of clouds. The windows from the house glowed with a yellow light. Hunter could see Mrs. Fowler and two of the boys through the kitchen window, finishing the dishes. They had missed dinner but Hunter knew there would be plenty of leftovers waiting for them.

They took care of the horses and the little calf, then walked across the moonlit yard to the lodge. Mrs. Fowler greeted them both with a bear hug.

"You boys sure do know how to worry a soul," she said with a look of mock consternation on her face. "Why didn't you tell me you were going on an overnight? I would have sent you more food."

"We didn't plan on it," said Smokey, grabbing a roll from the counter.

"Well, help yourself. I've got four meals covered and waiting for the two of you in the fridge. What do you want, breakfast, lunch or dinner?"

"How about all of them," answered Hunter with a wink of his eye.

Betsy Fowler noticed immediately the change in the boy's countenance. Something had happened to change him on their adventure. His pouting, sullen expression had been replaced by a warm, welcoming smile. She smiled back and looked quizzically at Smokey. Smokey just shrugged.

With his stomach full, Hunter hurried back to his cabin. He secretly hoped Julius wouldn't be there so he could write his letter in privacy. But Julius *was* there and eager to talk about Hunter's overnight trip in the desert. Hunter filled him in quickly then sent him out to the barn to check on the calf. While his cabin mate was gone, Hunter rummaged through his dresser until he found a pen and paper. He sat cross-legged on the patchwork quilt that covered his bed. Using a book for a portable desk, he set his pen to paper and started writing.

Dear Mom,

I am sorry that I have not written before now. I have been having a hard time learning to forgive and look at things from your point of view. The staff here has been great, especially Dr. Collins, Smokey and Mrs. Fowler. They have been patient with me and have been trying to help me. I admit that at first I was angry about being sent here but now I really like it. Please tell Grandpa 'Thank you' for paying for me to come here.

The best part about Promise Ranch is the horses. Smokey, he's the one in charge of the horses, has put me in charge of training one of them. She was a wild mustang and arrived the same time I did. I really love her and I think she loves me. I have been training her by doing everything that Smokey tells me to do. Yesterday, Smokey and I went for a long ride in the desert, looking for the herd of cattle. Sadly, we found a cow that was badly hurt and Smokey had to put her out of her misery. We brought her calf back to the ranch with us.

Last night we slept out under the stars. I couldn't sleep and I started thinking about how much the calf must miss its mother. Then it hit me like a truck: I miss you. I miss you so much, Mom. I am so sorry that I have hurt you. I promise to make it up to you. I promise to become the kind of man you always dreamt of me becoming. You will be proud of me someday.

Love,

Your son

P.S. Thanks for leaving my violin. I am teaching a younger boy how to play. He was doing great before his hand got broken. But that is another story.

Melody would not live to read the letter.

CHAPTER 23

Tragedy

SATURDAY WAS THE FIRST day of Christmas vacation for all the boys who had the freedom to come and go. Julius was up early packing things that he wanted for the holidays. Mr. Anderson was expected to arrive just after lunch to drive him to Salt Lake City for three weeks. Hunter was surprised at the sadness he felt as he thought of Julius leaving him. He hadn't realized, until now, how much he had come to rely on this tall, lanky kid for support. Thank goodness he would still have Sally.

After breakfast, Smokey assigned Julius and Hunter the task of driving his old pickup truck to the hay shed, filling it with hay and stacking it in the barn. Julius was a terrible driver. Everything was done with a jerk. Whether stopping, starting or turning, it didn't matter, he was just plain bad at it. The two boys soon dissolved into uncontrollable laughter. Through his tears born of merriment, Julius miraculously managed to get the truck to the hay shed.

Chucking bales of hay was easy for Hunter, now. Three months at the ranch had seen his body become strong, the muscles in his upper body looked like he had spent hours at the gym. *No need for a gym here,* he thought, *plenty of work to do.* With twenty bales stacked high in the bed of the pickup, the two boys climbed back into the cab.

Before attempting to get the truck into gear, Julius turned and looked squarely at Hunter.

Hunter felt himself squirm under the direct examination. "What?" he asked.

"I was just thinkin'. I'm sorry you're stuck here for Christmas."

Hunter shrugged. "It's okay. Yeah, it sucks, but I'll be okay. I'll bet Mrs. Fowler can cook up a great Christmas dinner, probably better than Thanksgiving."

Julius laughed. "That's about enough temptation to get me to stay!"

"And Smokey needs help with the horses and the new calf we brought in."

"Yeah. You're right there for sure."

"And Sally...she depends on me. Smokey says I'm her security blanket."

Julius chuckled. "That you are. Did you have a security blanket as a kid?"

"Not really, just my mom."

"I had this old blanket that I drug around with me until it looked like some sort of health hazard! My gram finally threw it away. Broke my heart. Never did forgive her." He smiled. Looking straight ahead, he added. "I saw the letter you wrote on your dresser...wasn't spying or anything."

Hunter shrugged. "That's okay."

"Proud of ya, bro."

"Thanks," Hunter whispered as he turned toward the window to hide the tears collecting in his eyes.

They jerked and jostled their way back to the barn in silence.

Right after lunch, Mr. Anderson pulled up to the lodge in his black BMW. He opened the door and unfolded his tall and slightly overweight body from the driver's seat. Hunter watched him from the window as the kind looking man stood up and squinted into the sun. A big smile filled Mr. Anderson's face when he saw Julius jogging toward him, his duffle bag in hand. Hunter could tell that Mr. Anderson genuinely liked the boy. Julius set the bag on the ground and the two embraced. A tinge of...what was it? Jealousy? Regret? Sorrow? Hunter couldn't tell, only that he hurt a bit inside.

Julius turned and, facing the window of the cabin where Hunter stood, beckoned him with a wave of his arm to come out. Hunter took a deep breath and stepped out of the cabin and across the yard.

Mr. Anderson proved to be just as Hunter imagined from the stories he had heard from Julius. It wasn't so much that he looked like Hunter had imaged. It was more that he *felt* like he had imagined. He felt like a father, a grandfather, a friend, all in one. The goodness in this man was obvious in the way he shook Hunter's hand and spoke to him. Yep, it was jealousy Hunter was feeling!

He stood and watched the car leave until even the dust the tires kicked up settled back to the ground. He walked over to Sally's pen

Hunter brushed her coat until it shone. He tacked her up and led her out of the paddock. He put one booted foot into the left stirrup and swung his other leg over her back. He marveled at how she just stood still and let him climb up onto her back. Settling into the western saddle, he took the reins in one hand the way Smokey had taught him and ran the palm of his other hand up and down her neck. She turned her head and her brown eyes seemed to twinkle. Hunter smiled to himself as he thought of the sadness that was once there. Clearly, it was gone.

Hunter rode down the dirt road that led from the ranch house to the entrance gate. He dismounted and looped the reins around one of the tall upright posts that supported the sign. He thought about the first time he had seen this sign. About the anger he felt as his grandpa drove under it. How different he felt now. Balancing carefully, he stepped across the cattle guard and up to the large metal mailbox. Opening the front, he pulled his letter out of his pocket and placed it inside. He shut the door and put up the red flag. He knew the rural route mail truck would not be by for a couple of days but he felt good that he had completed the task from his end.

That night, Mrs. Fowler recruited him and the other two boys who were staying at the ranch for the holidays. "Hey boys, I need some help getting this place ready for Christmas," she said, smiling and rosy cheeked like a real life Mrs. Santa Claus.

The little band of Christmas Elves tromped down the stairs to the basement where Betsy Fowler stored her decorations. Several trips up and down the stairs carrying heavy boxes were required, made easier with the Christmas music floating in the air. When the evening turned to night and the chores were complete, Mrs. Fowler and the boys sat in front of a blazing fire sending off the sweet smell of pinon pine logs, drinking hot chocolate, eating popcorn and marveling at the transformation that had taken place. The large log room suddenly felt much smaller and cozier. In the corner to the side of the big, stone fireplace, a ten-foot Christmas tree dazzled the eye. Bright lights twinkled all over it from top to bottom. A garland of lassoes wound their way through the cowboy-themed ornaments. Neckerchiefs were tied on the branches adding splashes of bright color. On the top, a large star shone like the star over Bethlehem.

While the tree was clearly the center of attention, there was not one place in the room that was bare of decorations. Wreaths hung in every window. Candle centerpieces graced every table. Even the old wooden cowboy on the front porch now wore a Santa hat and had a bag slung over his shoulder. It was beautiful and served to lift the spirits of the boys who were left behind when the others went home.

Hunter breathed in deeply, his lungs filling with the scent of fresh pine mixed with Mrs. Fowler's cinnamon candles. He lingered, not wanting to go back to his empty cabin just yet. Understanding, Mrs. Fowler brought him another cup of hot chocolate and a wreath to hang on the door of the M Lazy C cabin.

Monday should have been a fairly normal day. At least, it started out that way. There was extra work to do to cover for the missing boys. But Hunter didn't mind. Work kept his mind off home, his mom and even Julius.

Occasionally he would glance at his watch and wonder if the mail truck had been by to pick up his letter. He knew there would be a letter from her and he hoped it would be the last one she would have to write before she got his letter.

Hunter spent most of his chore-time in the barn with Smokey, feeding, mucking out stalls, taking care of the little orphaned calf.

"Want to go for a ride?" It was Smokey, a saddle hanging from each hand, stirrups dragging on the ground. This was, of course, a rhetorical question. The old cowboy already knew the answer. The answer was always the same when it came to Hunter and riding.

The two horsemen, now friends, headed out the back gate toward the mountains. Sally had become a great horse to ride, obedient and brave. She followed Hunter's directives without hesitation. They shuffled along at a slow jog for a while then broke into a rocking, ground-covering lope. Hunter breathed in deeply of the warm winter desert air. He gave Sally her head, and she picked her own sweet way around barrel and prickly pear cactuses and over rocky outcroppings. His mind was filled with thoughts of the night under the stars when he'd had such an awakening during his sleepless night. He hadn't shared the experience with Smokey, and he wondered if he should.

They stopped in the shade of a rocky ridge and dismounted to give Kit and Sally a rest. Smokey passed out some of his ever-present beef jerky and his canteen of water. Both tasted great to Hunter.

"Smokey, I feel different."

Smokey glanced over at him. "Yeah? What's different?"

"I have finally let go of my anger. I have forgiven my mom."

"Good choice, Pachelbel."

"Choice?" Hunter asked, confused.

"Yeah. Anger's a choice. Anger makes ya weak. So choosing it always hurts ya one way or the other. We get to choose how we will respond to every event and circumstance. Remember when I told ya 'bout the two sides of a horse's brain?"

"Yeah. The thinking side and the reacting side."

"That's right. Training the horse teaches him to think instead of just react. Well, with people, anger is one of those responses we use when we are just using our reacting side of the brain. Forgiveness takes a lot of thinkin' and choosin'."

Hunter nodded. That made sense in a cowboy wisdom sort of way.

"So, what are you going to do about it?"

"I already did. I wrote a letter to my mom."

A crooked smile appeared on Smokey's face, and he reached over and knocked Hunter's hat off his head. "Proud o' you boy. Right proud o' you."

Sally chose that moment to give Hunter a nudge with her head. Smokey erupted in laughter. "Guess Sally's proud o' ya, too!"

They mounted up and rode back to the ranch slowly, side by side. Smokey shared more of his cowboy wisdom and Hunter soaked it all up like a sponge. "Always wondered why people just notice the colors at the beginning and the end of a day and not the middle," Smokey mused. "Look around you now, Pachelbel. There're colors everywhere you look. Even the sky ain't just one shade 'o blue. And them rocks...reds, browns...all different."

Hunter smiled as he looked around, following Smokey's hand motions. The world *did* look more beautiful today than it had for a long time. His mind went back to the first time he drove under the "Promise Ranch" sign. At that time, all he saw was weeds and rocks and dirt. Now the entire desert looked alive with color. The lichen painted the tall rock face of the cliffs a vibrant shade of chartreuse. The tan sand and red slick rock took turns painting the desert floor in stripes. The cactus poked through the surface to give the whole landscape a curious texture. "Beauty is in the eye of the beholder," he whispered.

Smokey glanced over at him and smiled.

They rode into the ranch and directly to the barn where they unsaddled the horses, brushed them off and did the feeding. The little calf was eager to be fed so, after getting flakes of hay to the horses, Hunter fed the little orphan a big bottle of milk. Hunter smiled as he watched the calf drink down the whole bottle. As the calf pulled on the long nipple, Hunter looked around him. The barn in which they were keeping the calf was large and airy. Shafts of sunlight found their way between the barn boards, lighting the floating specks of dust. Straw and hay covered the ground. The smell of molasses-soaked feed and saddle soap mingled to create a lovely aroma...the cowboy's cologne. He sighed deeply, reveling in the contentment he felt.

The boy left the calf's stall, slapped the dust off his hat against his jeans, replaced it low over his brow and walked out of the barn.

Rounding the corner, he recognized the car immediately. An electric charge of excitement went through him. His grandfather was here!

Hunter broke into a run. Seeing him coming, his grandfather and Dr. Collins stepped out of the lodge. Hunter's excitement changed instantly to panic. The looks on their faces and the stiffness with which they moved told the boy that something was wrong. Terribly wrong. His grandpa looked dreadful. He had a couple days of stubble growing on his face. His eyes were sunken and had dark circles around them.

Hunter's grandpa opened his arms wide, inviting him in. Hunter stepped forward and let his grandpa envelop him. His heart was pounding loudly, so loudly he was sure Dr. Collins could hear it. His grandpa held on tightly and Hunter could feel his body shiver. Or was it his grandpa's body? He wasn't sure.

Dr. Collins gently directed the two of them into the lodge, across the large dining room and into his cozy office. Hunter and his grandpa were still clinging to each other though Hunter had no idea why.

"Hunter, we need you to sit down," said Dr. Collins in a voice devoid of his usual cheerfulness.

"What's this all about?" Hunter asked as he sat himself in the chair that Dr. Collins had motioned toward. His mouth was suddenly very dry and his muscles felt limp.

Just then, his grandfather burst into tears. Hunter snapped his head around and stared at him. He had never seen his strong and stoic grandfather cry and he had a hard time believing it, even as he watched him. The panic began to well up inside of him again, and he wished these adults would get right to the point. He felt beads of sweat form on his forehead and roll down the side of his face, past his ears and down his neck. He gripped the arms of the chair to hold himself in and forced himself to wait.

Dr. Collins stated the obvious. "Hunter, I'm afraid we have some terrible news for you."

Hunter slowly turned his head and looked directly into Dr. Collins's eyes. For the first time, he noticed what kind eyes the man had. But beneath the kindness, there was a layer of sorrow.

Foreboding filled Hunter's body, causing the muscles in his throat to constrict. He wanted to shout: "Tell me! Just tell me what's going on?" But the words got stuck in his throat like peanut butter.

Dr. Collins's eyes seemed to draw him in. Hunter wasn't sure if the words he heard were actually spoken aloud or if he could hear the counselor's thoughts.

Slowly the truth was revealed. "Your mother is dead...She was killed by your father...Your father appeared at her door, pounding and shouting in a drunken rage. The neighbors heard it all...They heard her let him in and the argument that ensued...They heard the sound of breaking glass, a scream, a gunshot, and then silence...The last thing they heard was the pounding footsteps of the man running past their door. They looked out in time to see him descend the stairway. There is no question who it was...who did it."

Dr. Collins gently fed him the sentences as one would feed a baby its first rice cereal. The man spared the boy the gruesome details, preferring just to get across the bare minimum of what had happened. He knew full well what damage words can do to a teenager's developing brain. Hunter didn't need that.

Words.

Brutal words.

They seem to have a life of their own and never die.

But some things don't go down gently no matter how careful you are. The words chased after Hunter, surrounding him, trapping him, like a cowboy's lasso. He felt like he was teetering on the edge of a precipice and would plunge down into the abyss at any minute.

Something happened within Hunter, something dark and terrible. It started deep in his chest. Then, like a tiny seed, it began to grow until it filled his entire body. A seed of hate. A seed of rage. A seed of revenge. It burst alive and spread throughout him until it consumed him completely.

A groan filled with pain arose from somewhere deep within Hunter, feeling like acid burning him as it came up. He collapsed forward, his forearms on his thighs, his hands clutching his knees. His grandfather, still weeping dropped to his knees in front of him and took his hands in his. Hunter felt his heart pounding in his chest as he gasped for breath. His entire body felt like it was caving in on itself. Soon there would be nothing left. That would be wonderful...to not even exist.

Dr. Collins pulled his chair up beside him. Hunter was not even aware that he was there until he felt the man's arm around his shoulder.

Still gasping for breath, he whispered, "When?" Even as he said it, he realized that it was a stupid question. What did it matter? When? She was dead, wasn't she? What difference did it make *when* it happened?

"Saturday night," said Dr. Collins softly.

Saturday night? Saturday night he had been helping Betsy Fowler put up Christmas decorations. He was laughing and having fun and his mother was being murdered! It all seemed so ironic. His body began shaking uncontrollably, and he jerked upright.

"If I'd been home with her, this wouldn't have happened!" he shouted. He glared at his grandfather. "It's your fault! If you hadn't sent me here, I could have been there to protect her." He shot the words from his mouth as though they were darts aiming for a target. In fact, they were, and the target was his grandfather's heart.

The words hit their mark. His grandfather could not respond. He didn't have the strength. He could only look at the floor and weep.

Hunter knew he was being spiteful but he didn't care. He wanted to hurt someone, and words were his only weapon.

Suddenly he snapped. He jerked his hands away and stood up. Hunter felt that if he stayed there for one minute longer, he would explode. Right there in that very room he would burst into a million pieces. He ran to the door, jerked it open and left.

His grandfather stood up and started after him but Dr. Collins stopped him. "Let him be alone for a while," the doctor said.

Betsy Fowler stood in the doorway of the kitchen and watched Hunter go. Black streaks of mascara painted her face.

The last time Hunter tried to run from his pain, it hadn't worked out very well for him. But he was not thinking about that right now.

He was incapable of logical reasoning at the moment. He was only reacting and all he wanted was to get away. And he knew right where he was going. He was going to find his father.

CHAPTER 24

Seeking Revenge

HUNTER HAD SPENT ENOUGH time in the desert with Smokey to know that survival depended upon preparation. With his brow furrowed and his jaw set, he grabbed his backpack from his closet and threw in a change of clothes, some bottles of water and granola bars, fruit and trail mix from his supply in his dresser. He quickly gathered up what little money he had and put it in one of the front zipper pockets. He placed a flashlight in one of the side pockets.

Outside, the sky was darkening as thick heavy rain clouds covered the sun. The wind began blowing, bringing the scent of predators with it. Hunter slung the pack over his shoulder and headed out the door. Looking out to the west, he noticed the dark clouds rolling toward the ranch. Not to be deterred, he returned to his room, stuffed in a rain poncho and left the cabin.

Hunter had one last task that he needed to do before he started on his journey. With long, determined strides, he headed to the barn. Mustang Sally saw him coming and let out a loud whinny. "Quiet girl," Hunter whispered. "I don't need anyone to know I'm here," he added as he looked toward the open barn door, hoping that Smokey would not see him.

The young teen opened the gate and went into Sally's paddock. She walked over to him and blew warm air into his face. Hunter smiled, and he felt his throat constrict and tears sting his eyes. He fell into her chest and wrapped both arms around her neck. He let himself cry. Sally tucked her head in a horse's version of a hug and stood there as though trying to absorb his pain as best she could.

When his tears were spent, Hunter stepped back. He ran his hands down her face and cupped her muzzle in his hands. He gazed into the deep brown pools that were her eyes. Those eyes. The ones that captured him the first time he saw her. The ones that pulled his heart into hers.

He felt the wind start up again, coming from the west. Wind has a way of irritating and agitating both humans and animals. When it is bringing in a storm, it also motivates both to get moving. With great effort, he pulled himself away from her eyes and glanced behind her at the approaching storm. "I've got to go now, Sally. Don't worry about me. I will be back for you someday...you can count on that." He leaned forward and pressed his forehead between those eyes. Then Hunter spun around and dashed out the gate, letting it bang shut behind him.

Once out of Sally's paddock, the boy took a moment to get his bearings. He knew he had to go in a northeasterly direction to reach Rattlesnake Gulch and the bus station he had seen on his one visit to the little town. Remembering his geometry, he said to himself, "The shortest distance between two points is a straight line." After one last look at Sally, he turned and started running. The wind carried Sally's neighs to him as she beckoned him to return. He forced himself to keep going.

Dark clouds moved rapidly in from the west like a movie on fast forward. As they rolled and tumbled over one another, flashes of lightning streaked from one cloud to the next, spilling over to the ground. Perhaps it was the ferocity of the storm that prompted Dr. Collins, Betsy Fowler and Hunter's grandpa to decide that it was time to go check on the boy. Time to give him shelter from the storms all around him.

The wind caught the screen door as they left the lodge, causing it to bang violently against the wooden Indian as the aged statue stood and smiled, daring the storm to touch him even as the wind picked up his Santa hat and blew it across the yard. The three adults raised their arms across their faces in a futile attempt to shield themselves from the wind and pelting rain as they splashed through the quickly forming puddles. By the time they crossed the yard and stepped up onto the porch in front of the cabin named "M Lazy C," all three were soaked to the core.

Dr. Collins rapped on the door of the cabin. "Hunter," he shouted in order to be heard over the bellowing wind. "Hunter, may we come in?" Silence answered them. "Hunter, may we come in, please?" the doctor repeated.

Silence.

"Hunter, it's your grandpa. Can I come in and sit with you?"

Silence.

The three adults looked back and forth at one another.

"He's not there!" exclaimed Betsy Fowler. "I can feel it in my bones." She reached for the doorknob and jerked open the door. The three of them pushed their way in, being propelled by the wind. Once inside, they stopped and looked around.

Empty.

Hunter was not there.

"Where could he be?" asked Hunter's grandpa.

"There's nothing he loves more than that horse. Maybe he's down by the barn," suggested Betsy Fowler.

When they arrived at the barn, the only thing they saw in Sally's pen was a very agitated mustang mare. The little dun mustang was running back and forth in her pen, her head and tail high, her eyes directed toward the east, her loud whinnies and squeals nearly drowned out by the thunder, her black legs getting coated with mud.

Dr. Collins shouted through the wind and rain. "Let's go find Smokey. Maybe he's seen him."

The three worried adults ran to the barn and struggled against the wind to open the door. After much effort, they stepped inside. The wind blowing through the gaps in the barn boards kicked up the dust and pieces of hay. They had a hard time seeing anything at first. Betsy Fowler sneezed several times.

"Who's there?" Smokey's voice came from the tack room.

"Just us," shouted Dr. Collins.

Smokey stepped to the doorway, a bridle in one hand, a bit in the other. "What are you folks doin' out in this storm?" asked the cowboy, with a grin and a twinkle in his eyes revealing that he was really glad for the company.

Dr. Collins motioned toward the man standing beside him. "This is Hunter's grandfather William Mitchell. Have you seen the boy?"

"No. Why?" Smokey could tell by the looks in their eyes that something was terribly wrong.

Dr. Collins and Betsy Fowler took turns rehearsing the events that had transpired while William Mitchell stood and wept.

Smokey's grin changed instantly. His lips pursed, and he rubbed the stubble on his wrinkled chin. "He's on the run."

"On the run? Where on earth would he run to?" asked Betsy Fowler, panic in her voice. Smokey shook his head. "Is Sally in her pen?"

"Yes, that's where we checked first," replied Dr. Collins. "She's agitated but she's there."

"Then he must have headed to the road. Maybe looking for a ride," responded Smokey. The four adults ran through the wind and rain to Grandpa Mitchell's car. Hunter's grandpa, his hands shaking, struggled to insert the key in the ignition. Finally successful, he turned the key and the engine started with a roar. William Mitchell turned the car and headed down the dirt road, swerving and sliding in the mud. When the car went under the ranch sign, he stopped. Turning his head from side to side and squinting to see through the beating windshield wipers he said, "Which way?"

Smokey was the only one with a guess. "I took him to Rattlesnake Gulch once. That's to the left. Let's try that."

"He can't have gotten far," said Betsy, the worry evident in her voice.

"Unless he was picked up..." Dr. Collins let the rest of his thought hang in the air. Everyone finished it in their own minds.

Hunter's grandpa turned the car to the left and headed toward Rattlesnake Gulch.

While the adults drove up the road, Hunter ran across the desert, his footprints quickly dissolving in the rain. He had a strong internal compass and kept himself moving, as quickly as he was able, to the northeast. His legs and lungs both started to ache but he kept going, letting his anger drive him forward.

The surface of the paddock was getting muddier and slipperier as Sally ran back and forth. At times she had trouble staying on her feet. Her heart was pounding. Her body was soaking from both the rain and her own sweat. Her nostrils flared, sucking in air that went right out in loud, mournful whinnies. Her eyes were opened wide, the dark brown irises outlined with white. The other horses around her were becoming increasingly restless by her behavior as well. Had Smokey been there, he would have had his hands full trying to calm them. But Smokey was not there. At this moment, he was in a car that was being driven toward the nearest town.

Time did not calm Sally. If anything, she was becoming more anxious. She started bucking and kicking at the fence boards. Two powerful back legs began hammering at the brittle, sun-bleached wood. Kick after kick was directed at the fence. Pieces of splintered wood flew through the air, carried on the wind. Eventually, the fence proved to be more of a discouragement than a barrier. When the top two boards came crashing down toward the outside of the pen, Sally stopped and examined her work. Pleased with herself, she circled the muddy pen once more, this time at a canter, and headed for the break in the fence. With one strong push from her hindquarters, she lifted her body up and over the lower boards of the broken fence.

She didn't take time to revel in her success. Instead she lifted her head and started galloping in the direction she had seen her boy go. The horses that were left behind called after her, but she did not answer. She was on a mission.

As she ran, her ears twitched forward and back, searching for sounds. Her nostrils flared. Sally breathed deeply, taking in the earthy smell of the damp desert. Her eyes searched the horizon in front of her. She had to find her boy. There was danger out here. She could feel it. She could smell it. And soon, she was sure, she would see it.

CHAPTER 25

Danger in the Desert

HUNTER RAN THE ENTIRE time the storm raged, helped along by the wind at his back. The desert wilderness through which he ran was barren, punctuated with rocks and boulders and colored with pinon pines and cactus. With the storm right on top of him, all of his surroundings were colored in shades of black and gray, lit only in the strobe light-like flashes of lightning. The storm was moving the same northeasterly direction but much faster than Hunter could run. Soon, it was ahead of him, and the wind and rain stopped their beating.

The storm blew over him in a little under an hour, the clouds lifting off the western horizon enough to let the late-day sun light the clouds from beneath and shine on the eastern cliffs. Hunter kept his eyes on them as he moved on, step after heavy step, the golden light surrounding him. Finally, he could move no further. He stopped, bent over and grabbed his knees, sucking in great gulps of freshly washed desert air. The salty drips of sweat stung his eyes as they worked their way between his lashes. He lifted a hand and rubbed his eyes, only serving to make matters worse. He grumbled under his breath as he stood up and started jogging again.

Eventually, Hunter became convinced that he was far enough away from the ranch that anyone looking for him would have a hard time finding him. So he slowed his pace to a determined walk, feeling his boots squish into the wet sandy soil as he stomped along. Finally deciding that the stomping took too much energy, he just started walking. As he moved forward, the images of what he imagined his mother must have gone through kept filling his mind and he shook his head to try to dislodge them.

Images.

Brutal Images.

Rising around him like flood-waters.

He pressed his hand against his forehead, trying to push them away. He forced his eyes to stay open and tried to focus on the ridge ahead, the line of cliffs he had set as his target as the place to stop for the night.

The little stream that trickled down through the canyon had been feed by the rains until now it had swelled into a rushing river. When Hunter reached its banks, he realized he would have to turn north at this point until the swollen river passed.

As he walked along, he felt the sun on the side of his face, bathing him in warmth and pushing him forward. "Hurry," it seemed to say. "I will be leaving you soon. Hurry." Hunter quickened his pace.

The wind was now reduced to a whisper. "Where are you going? Where are you going?" it murmured as it rustled the twigs on the cottonwood trees that lined the creek bed.

"I'm going to avenge my mother," Hunter shouted back at it. "She needed me, and I wasn't there!" A moan lifted from deep within him, and his eyes clouded with tears again. "I wasn't there," he sobbed and collapsed to the ground. He buried his face in his crossed arms. His body shook as he sobbed.

The distraught boy sensed that he was not alone before he heard or saw anything. Anyone alone in the desert can sense the presence of an unwelcome companion, large or small. As he gasped for breath, sucking in the rapidly cooling air, he heard a low, deep growl. He raised his head and looked into the malevolent yellow eyes of a malnourished coyote. The eyes were more wolf than dog. A chill ran the length of Hunter's spine. Frantic, he scrambled to his feet. It was then that he noticed three other coyotes standing to his side. His whole body began trembling and he took several long, deep breaths to calm himself. Forcing oneself to be calm is never easy but he was sure that panicking would not help.

Hunter bent down, picked up several rocks and stood back up, trying to make himself look as big as possible. The boy started throwing them. "No! Get away!" he shouted, repeating it with each throw. One rock hit its mark, right between the animal's eyes. It yelped and ran a short distance before circling to the back of the group...but not leaving. The pack of coyotes became more restless and moved back and forth, letting out sharp, high-pitched barks. They seemed to be communicating with one another as they repositioned themselves on three sides of Hunter, forcing him to continually spin around.

Hunter picked up more rocks and threw them again, some hitting, some missing, but none convincing the vicious, hungry animals to leave. He turned and started running toward the cliffs. *Protection*, he thought to himself. *Like the early Indian tribes. If I can reach the cliffs, I can climb to safety.*

He pumped his arms to get more power and move his body forward. The tormented and frightened boy ran as fast as he could but he could not outrun the coyotes. He was learning the hard lesson that anger weakens you.

He could hear the pack of coyotes howling as their padded feet patted the ground and splashed through the puddles that had formed on the slick rock. They seemed to just keep pace with him, as though confident that they had the upper hand and didn't need to exert themselves too much.

Hunter felt his heart pounding and his lungs burning as he forced himself to keep running. He kept his eyes on the cliff ahead, hopeful that it would provide the refuge he sought: the cliff dwellings Smokey told him about on their trip into Rattlesnake Gulch.

Just before the sun sank below the western horizon, Hunter reached the cliffs. Ahead of him loomed one of the most amazing sights he had ever seen. Centuries earlier, a series of caves had been dug into the cliff wall at various heights. Some were embellished with pueblo structures, doorways, windows and square walls. All were accessed by spindly ladders made from lengths of thin, straight poles, crossed with smaller ones, and lashed together with leather strips. On any other occasion, it would have been fascinating to explore the caves. Today, all Hunter desired was to get into one, and fast!

The coyote pack seemed to sense where their prey was going and started howling and running faster in an attempt to cut him off from his intended escape route. Hunter reached the first ladder just as the coyotes reached him. With the wild beasts nipping at his heels and their hot breath burning him, he leapt onto the ladder, connecting with it several feet off the ground. He grabbed the sides of the ladder and placed a foot on the fourth or fifth rung. The storm had left the wood wet and slippery, and his boot slipped off. He felt a sharp tooth cut through the leather of his boot. His foot slipped out of the boot, leaving it behind in the coyote's mouth. His arms tensed as he pulled himself up, his feet struggling for a foothold. Just as he thought his arms would give out, Hunter felt his foot connect with a solid rung, and he started scrambling up the ladder.

The coyotes raced around the base of the ladder howling, angry that their dinner might be getting away. Hunter paused for a few minutes, perched in the middle of the ladder. He needed to catch his breath. He held on and looked down at the coyotes who continued to pace back and forth below, yelping and crying, their howls amplified by the stone walls of the cliff.

Hunter turned his head and looked up toward the top of the ladder where it rested against a stone ledge. The shelf ran in front of a cave dwelling, the perfect spot for the night. He started climbing up the ladder again.

The boy had nearly reached the top when the rung he put all his weight on cracked and broke just as he let go with his hand to reach up to the top rung of the ladder. Before he even realized what was happening, Hunter felt himself falling. All the way down he screamed. He heard the bone break the minute he hit the ground.

Hunter landed in a crumpled heap at the base of the ladder. The slick rock on which he fell offered no cushion to soften his fall. The angle at which he hit the ground caused his femur in his upper right leg to break, sending the lower portion jutting out through the skin of his thigh.

The stab of pain made Hunter immediately both queasy and dizzy. Never had he felt such all-consuming pain. His brain was having a hard time registering just what had happened. All it could process was the pain pulsing throughout his body. Hunter let out a loud cry and began gasping for breath, moaning loudly between each shallow intake of air. His body began shaking.

The coyotes scattered as the boy fell, frightened by the primal scream coming from their prey. But they didn't go far. As soon as the boy landed and their keen ears picked up the moan of pain and fear, they turned and looked at him, their yellow eyes glowing in the gathering dusk. He was theirs and they knew it.

The leader of the pack stepped cautiously forward, sniffing the air. The wild animal's lips curled above sharp teeth and fangs. A low, threatening growl left his throat. He stopped and sniffed the air again. He could detect the scent of blood. The saliva dripped from his jowls.

Hunter looked up and his heart beat loudly within him. Gritting his teeth, he attempted to slide his body back. With a loud yelp of pain, he collapsed behind the ladder. "Oh God, please help me," he cried to the heavens. He sobbed and looked back to the ground. "I'm not worthy of your help," he whispered. This was one thing he was sure of. He covered his head and waited for the attack to begin that would end this pain. In the forefront of his thoughts, he decided that this was as good a place to suffer, and maybe die, as any.

CHAPTER 26

Sally's Battle

NO HUMANS AND FEW creatures heard Hunter's cry. But the only one that really mattered did. Mustang Sally, her sides heaving and heart pounding wildly, kept running and searching through the storm. Now that the wind and rain had passed, she looked frantically from side to side. With her eyes on the side of her head, a slight turn of just ten degrees one way then the other enabled her to see in a three hundred and sixty degree circle. She knew that Hunter was out there somewhere but she had no idea where...until she heard the scream.

The little mustang mare's ears pivoted to the left. She turned her body and began running toward where the sound had come. Darkness was falling fast, but the mare could still see the outlines of the cliffs ahead with their black apertures at various heights carved into the stone face. They made the wall look like it had eyes, eyes watching and threatening her.

As Sally drew nearer, her eyes picked up the shapes of the four coyotes. Her ears pricked forward until she realized what was happening. Then they pressed tightly backward. Her nostrils flared and she bared her teeth. The little mare lowered her head and charged.

Horses are not predators; they are prey animals. Their instinctive response to danger is to run, which is why they have such long legs. However, when cornered or desperate, they will fight. This is what Sally was prepared to do now. She was desperate. Her mind filled with images of an earlier encounter with coyotes. Images that were extremely painful. Once before, she had faced a pack of coyotes. They had taken her colt from her. She would not let that happen again. The images drove her forward in desperation.

Images.

Brutal Images.

Swirling around her like wind whipped sage brush.

So focused were they on their approach to their wounded prey, the coyotes didn't even realize Sally was coming until she was upon them. The first coyote Sally reached was the smallest of the pack and no contest for Sally's strong teeth and jaws. She headed in a beeline for the wild dog and reached her side in a matter of just a few long, powerful strides. She arched her neck, lowered her head and clamped her teeth around the coyote's neck. She lifted it high in the air and threw it down to the ground like a dirty old rag. Oblivious to the yelps of pain coming from her quarry, she reared up on her hind legs and rammed her sharp front hooves into the animal's ribs. It yelped no more.

The other three coyotes stopped their advance and turned, the coarse hairs rising on their backs. As if working in concert, they curled their lips, growled and slunk low to the ground. The largest of the pack walked stealthily straight forward, growling softly. The other two split apart and moved to either side of the approaching horse, their new enemy an enemy that needed to be dealt with before they could have the feast they were craving.

Hearing the cries of the first coyote, Hunter lifted his head. His eyes had trouble focusing through the waves of pain. The images seemed to sway and move in and out of clarity. He tried to steady them by pressing his knuckles against his eyes. For a brief moment, all became clear. A few yards away stood Sally, stomping and snorting and shaking her mane. She seemed to be taunting the three coyotes, daring them to come after her.

Hunter summoned what little strength he had and pushed himself up on his arms. "Sally! No! Go away! Get out of here! Salle-e-e-e!" he cried as the three coyotes left their crouching positions and leaped toward her.

Sally reared and let out a loud neigh before lowering her front legs and whirling around. She kicked both hind feet viciously at one coyote, sending him rolling across the sandy ground. The injured animal struggled to his feet, shook his head and tried with difficulty to gain his bearings.

Meanwhile, the other two coyotes were stopped in their advance only momentarily. They moved to either side, their jaws snapping at the mare's legs. Sally moved around quickly to avoid getting bitten. One of the coyotes leaped to the little horse's back and clamped its teeth into her neck. She let out a high-pitched scream and fell to the ground in an attempt to crush her attacker. The coyote jumped off her back just before she landed, spun around and attacked again. From her prone position, Sally had only her legs for defense. She kicked at the approaching coyote, striking him between the eyes. He collapsed.

The second coyote saw her time to strike. With the mare down on her side, the coyote ran forward. Sally struggled to get up and was in a sitting position when the coyote ripped into her chest. The mare cried out in pain as she tried to get her legs underneath her so she could stand. But the coyote held on, even once she was on her feet, dangling from a large flap of skin. Sally arched her neck and bit at the coyote until it let go. With blood streaming down her legs, she stomped her attacker until it moved no more.

Her sides heaving, blood and sweat flowing down her legs, Mustang Sally turned on her next would-be attacker. She lowered her head, glared at the last standing coyote and snorted. The coyote howled and yelped then turned and ran. Sally neighed by way of a threat as though warning it not to come back. Slowly, she turned back around to face Hunter and her legs crumpled beneath her. With a groan, she laid over on her side.

Hunter watched in horror as his beloved horse fell to her side. "NO-O-O-O-O!" he screamed. "Sally! Get up! Go home! Smokey will help you. Please get up!" He started sobbing. "No Sally! You can't die!"

The injured teen shook his head violently. If she was going to die, he wasn't going to let her die alone. He had to find a way to get to her. To be with her. They could die together.

He started pulling himself across the slick rock upon which he had landed. It sloped down and he started sliding. The pain from his broken leg felt like a grenade had exploded within him. He was sure this was the end. He was sure that, once and for all, he would not live through this. His screaming echoed off the canyon walls and sent a crow flying away, cawing to the night stars. But he kept going, sliding on his side across the sandy soil, determined to reach Sally. A streak of blood formed beneath him as he scooted along, soaking into the sand but leaving a dark red stain, a line marking his path. As he struggled along, moving forward only an inch at a time, he told himself that if she was going to die then he would die with her. That was the only motivation that kept him going.

He pulled himself with his arms, digging his fingers into the soil like a rake. He pushed with his one good leg. Ahead he could see Sally on her side, her ribcage moving up and down slowly but rhythmically. Her eyes were closed. A stream of blood, looking like black ink in the darkness, dripped from her nostrils and sank into the sand. A river of blood flowed from the deep gash in her chest.

After what seemed like a lifetime, Hunter reached her head. He put his arms around it and laid his cheek against her jaw. "Sally, oh Sally," he gasped. The cold was climbing out of the ground as though it had been hiding there just waiting for him. He pressed his body against the mare's back for warmth.

The body shuts down when the pain gets too bad.

CHAPTER 27

The Rescue

FINDING A BOY LOST in the desert could be compared to the proverbial needle in a haystack. The fact that Hunter was found so quickly could only be called a miracle.

When there was no sign of him anywhere around the small town of Rattlesnake Gulch, William Mitchell, Betsy Fowler, Smokey, and Dr. Collins rushed back to the ranch, calling friends and fellow ranchers the whole drive back. When they pulled up to the ranch house, several men and women were waiting for them on horseback. Betsy hustled around, gathering and distributing flashlights, blankets, water and food to all the rescuers.

Everyone had satellite cell phones for communication in the wilderness.

Smokey immediately took command of the operation. He divided the riders into teams and sent them off in different directions. It wasn't until Smokey went to the barn to saddle up his own horse that he noticed the broken fence around Sally's pen and that Sally was gone. The deep hoof prints in the sandy soil were still fairly easy to follow. But would they lead him to Hunter? He had no way of knowing for sure...he just had a hunch that they would, and cowboys have learned to follow their hunches.

Smokey and a neighbor took off to the east, racing the sun as it sank into the western sky. As it did so, it lit the storm clouds to the east from beneath with an eerie greenish light.

Initially, the hoof prints were easy to follow but as they traveled further, they rode across some stretches of slick rock. No hoof prints were visible on the hard surface of the rock.

"Spread out but keep moving east. Yell if you pick up her hoof prints," commanded Smokey. Time and again, this method worked, and they kept progressing eastward.

They reached the little creek that had forced Hunter to turn north. The storm-caused river of water had passed, leaving its mark with waves in the sand of the wash. But no foot or hoof prints could be seen by the searchers.

The first few times they lost track of Sally's trail they were able to find it again fairly quickly. But this time, they searched and found nothing. Whether the wind and rain had washed them away or she had stayed on the slick rock, they didn't know. Another thing they didn't know was just how close they were to where Hunter lay broken on the earth and where Sally slowly stalked a vicious pack of coyotes. That was the miracle part.

The two horsemen stopped their search when the desert silence was broken by the distant sound of coyotes howling and a horse screaming a high-pitched neigh. The noise was greatly amplified as it bounced off the cliff walls. The wild sounds were carried on the softening breezes to the cowboys. They looked at each other then toward the cliffs.

"That must be Sally! Sounds like she's in trouble," Smokey said. They headed to the north as fast as they dared in the fading light of day. The last thing they needed was to have a horse put a foot in a hole and break a leg! The sounds disappeared as a crow eerily cawed in the darkness overhead.

Smokey and his neighbor, long-time Arizona rancher Duane Kirkmeyer, arrived at the cliff dwellings, the scene of the bloody battle, to find Sally lying on her side and Hunter unconscious, lying with his head on top of hers. Neither one was aware of their arrival. Neither one had much more time to live. That was obvious from the amount of blood that colored the sand around their broken and torn bodies.

Smokey leapt from his horse and ran to Hunter, examining his body as he moved up to him. He knelt in the sand beside him and checked for a pulse. With relief, he found one. Weak, yes, but at least it was there.

"Hey, bring me a blanket, Duane! Quick!" he shouted to his friend. The old rancher did as requested. Slowly, gently, Smokey slid Hunter off Sally and onto the blanket, covering him tightly to keep him warm. Then he bowed his head and said a prayer.

While Smokey worked on Hunter, Duane Kirkmeyer called for help. A life-flight helicopter was dispatched, cutting across the desert with its *whomp, whomp* sound. At the first sound of the helicopter blades cutting through the air, Sally lifted her head and neighed. Her eyes opened so wide that the dark brown irises were ringed with white. Her body started shaking, and she struggled to get up. To her, the sound brought back the frightening memories of that day in the prairie when she and her herd were rounded up by the terrifying giant insect.

"Hold the horse, Duane," Smokey yelled over the beating blades and the machine-made sandstorm.

One man against a panicking horse, even a severely injured horse, is not a fair fight. Sally got to her feet and stumbled over to the cliff, neighing wildly. Incapable of running, she pressed her body against the stone wall and continued snorting and neighing, all the time looking from the monster to the prone body of Hunter and back again. She struggled to move toward them when she saw the humans put Hunter into the body of the huge insect. In her mind, she had saved her boy from one threat only to have him consumed by another. She stumbled and wove from side to side as she worked her way toward the black helicopter. She stopped suddenly and watched with fear as it rose into the air, taking Hunter with it. Her devoted heart went with it as well.

Overflowing with grief and pain, Mustang Sally collapsed to the ground, content to die.

Duane Kirkmeyer walked quickly to his saddlebag and pulled out a rifle. He walked up to the mare and placed the barrel against her temple. She didn't move, not even when he cocked the Winchester.

The "oomph" from the man and the "bang" from the gun went off at the same time. The rancher found himself on the ground, looking into Smokey's angry eyes.

"What do ya think yer doing?" shouted Smokey.

"Gonna put the little nag outta her misery. What are you doin' on top of me?"

"You kill that horse and the boy dies. I know it as sure as I'm sittin' here."

"Sittin' here on top of me!"

Smokey climbed off his buddy. "Sorry. But I can't let you kill Sally. She's been Hunter's life-line for three months and she still is. I need to save her to save him."

Duane Kirkmeyer got up and brushed the sand from his shirt and pants. "Whatever you say, Smokey. But she ain't goin' ta make it anyway. Seems to me yer just makin' her suffer fer no reason."

Smokey knelt at Sally's side, stroking her neck. "She'll make it. I'll make sure of that. She's saved that boy twice. Now we need to save her...but I'll need the boy's help to do it."

CHAPTER 28

Healing the Boy

THE BOY WOKE UP in the ICU, alone except for the beeping machines all around him. He was not experienced at hospital stays, and a surge of panic ran through him. He jerked his head from side to side, hoping to see someone. The door to his room was slightly ajar, and the boy could hear someone talking somewhere beyond the doorway.

"Hey!" Hunter said, his voice sounding like a frog croaking. "Hey! Is anyone out there?" he said, this time with a little more clarity and volume.

The talking stopped and was replaced with the sound of footsteps on linoleum. A young Hispanic woman in a pair of bright pink scrubs opened the door and peeked around the frame. "Well, well. Look whose back among the living," she said with a thick Mexican accent. She stepped into the room and up to the side of his bed. "How are you feeling?"

"Where am I? What am I doing here?" Hunter protested as he started to raise himself up on his elbows. A sharp pain shot through his body and he fell back with a cry.

"Easy, amigo. You're not ready to go anywhere yet."

"What happened to me?"

"You have a compound fracture of your right femur," she said suddenly sounding all business. "The doctors have set it, but you are going to be laid up for quite a while."

Hunter raised his head and looked down at his leg. It was wrapped in a cast from his hip to his ankle. A series of straps held it up off the bed. He looked around and noticed a tube in his arm that ran up to a bag into which a clear liquid was dripping. Wires ran from his chest to some sort of monitor. Another bag was collecting urine. He suddenly felt very claustrophobic, trapped by wires and machines.

Memories began flooding his brain, images that stung and weakened. Thoughts of his mother filled his mind. His throat constricted and he struggled to get a breath. He clutched his throat with his hands and tried to calm the tremors that racked his body

The nurse patted his shoulder and wiped the sweat off his forehead with a soft cloth. "You are at the University Medical Center Hospital in Tucson."

"How did I get here?" Hunter whispered

"You were brought in by Life Flight."

"When?"

"Two days ago."

Two days? He had been unconscious for *two days*?

The nurse patted his hand as a sign that she understood his confusion. "Let me go get the doctor. He'll be pleased that you're awake. He can answer all of your questions." She left the room, leaving him alone with the machines and his fears.

Sally? Sally what had happened to Sally? He let go of the tears he had been holding in while the nurse was in the room.

A few minutes later, a young doctor came in to see him. He had a neatly trimmed beard that covered dimples when he smiled, which was often. "Good morning," he said, kindly, as he snatched a tissue out of the box and handed it to Hunter to wipe his tears. He was wise enough not to mention them.

Hunter looked up at him but didn't respond as he dabbed his cheeks and blew his nose.

"I'm so glad to see you awake, dude. You've put that body through quite an ordeal. I'm not sure how much you remember but you came to us in a pretty bad state. You had lost a lot of blood, not to mention a badly broken femur. You are now the proud owner of a titanium rod and lots of screws. The airport security people aren't going to like you!" he said with a warm smile that brought wrinkles to the sides of his eyes. "Do you remember what happened out there?" the doctor said, patting his hand. Hunter didn't have the energy to move it.

"I was climbing the ladder to get away from the coyotes. The ladder broke..." the tears started again.

"Ah...that explains it. That's pretty hard rock to fall onto. Luckily for you, it was a clean break right in the middle of the bone. You're going to be in a lot of pain for at least a week.

We'll keep you here for several days on meds to control the pain."

"Sally?" Hunter whispered.

"What's that?"

"My horse...Sally."

"Oh...yes. Well, I really don't know. I just heard she was torn up pretty badly. Got the worst of those coyotes, I expect. There's someone here who can answer that. Your grandpa and Mrs. Fowler have been by your side nearly every minute. They just stepped out to get something to eat. I expect them back soon. They'll be mighty glad to see you back in the land of the living."

As the doctor was speaking, Mrs. Fowler and his grandpa walked in the door. Mrs. Fowler squealed with delight when she saw Hunter awake. "Hunter! Oh Hunter!" She rushed over to his bedside and took his face gently in her hands. "Welcome back!" Her face changed instantly from a beaming smile to a frown. "You gave us quite a fright, I don't mind telling you!" Her attempt to be stern was belied by the twinkle in her eyes.

"How are you feeling, son?" his grandpa asked in his typical gentle manner, his eyes filled with concern and a deep sadness.

Hunter looked up at him. His first thoughts were of his mother but his first words were of Sally. "Sally...Sally saved my life. She fought off the coyotes."

His grandpa nodded, pensively. "I 'spected as much."

"How is she?"

Grandpa shook his head. "When Smokey and his friend found the two of you, you were both in pretty bad shape. Lost a lot of blood. They called the life flight for you but Smokey's friend felt the most humane thing for Sally was to put her out of her misery."

"NO-O-O-O-O!" cried Hunter as he struggled to sit up.

His grandpa held up his hand. "Take it easy, son. Smokey wouldn't let him do it. He got the vet out there to anesthetize her and brought her back to the ranch in a trailer."

Hunter could feel his pounding heart relax a little as he lay back against the pillow.

"But it's not over yet," his grandpa cautioned. "She was very close to death. Smokey is determined to bring her back to health, but I don't want you to be too optimistic."

Hunter turned and looked up at the ceiling. "She will live," he whispered. "She saved my life. She has to live. She just has to."

Mrs. Fowler patted his shoulder. "We all hope so. Everyone is praying for her."

The next day, Dr. Collins came in to see him. "Hey Hunter!" he said enthusiastically as he walked in the door.

"Hi, Dr. Collins," Hunter responded without returning the enthusiasm.

Dr. Collins picked up on that immediately. "Not having such a good day?"

Hunter turned his head and looked blankly out the window. "Would you be? Anyone or any*thing* that gets close to me ends up getting hurt or dying."

"Explain to me why the terrible tragedies that have happened are your fault?"

"Well isn't it obvious?" turning back to face the counselor.

"Not to me," Dr. Collins said sincerely, cocking his head to one side.

"Let me spell it out for you," Hunter said in a distinctly AT manner. He looked up at the ceiling, a bit embarrassed at his own behavior but not willing to apologize. "My mom is dead all because I wasn't there."

"How could your being there have possibly changed anything?"

"I could have protected her!" Hunter said, snapping his head back toward Dr. Collins and giving him his best threatening glare.

Dr. Collins gave a little shrug. "You don't know that. Maybe you could have. But maybe not."

"I *could* have! And now Sally is probably going to die, too. All because of me!" He pressed his lips tightly together, clenched his fists and pounded the bed.

"Tell me why you were out there."

"I was heading to the bus station in Rattlesnake Gulch. And as soon as I can get out of here, I'm going to find my father."

"And do what?"

Hunter shook his head. He really hadn't thought that far. "I don't know. But somehow I will make him pay for what he did."

"Revenge?"

"Yeah. Revenge."

"Why not let the justice system do its job?"

"Sometimes revenge *is* justice."

"Remember when Smokey told you about the two sides of the horse's brain, the reacting side and the thinking side?"

Hunter looked steadily at Dr. Collins and didn't answer. It didn't require a response. He knew what he meant. The energy from his outburst dissipated, and Hunter felt like his insides were caving in. He turned his head and looked back out the window.

Had Hunter looked, it would have been obvious that Dr. Collins's heart ached for him. The slacked expression on his face and the dull eyes showed clearly that the counselor was extremely saddened by the terrible events Hunter was going through. Dr. Collins sighed deeply in an attempt to relieve some of the pain he was feeling for the boy.

"It's not fair!" moaned Hunter before bursting into tears.

Dr. Collins sat down on the chair beside Hunter's bed and rubbed the boy's shaking shoulders. "Life isn't fair for anyone...That's what makes it fair," the counselor whispered.

Over the next few days, Hunter spent a lot of time in the thinking side of his brain. Actually, being tied to a bed left him with little choice. His thoughts and Dr. Collins's counsel mixed together and marinated in his mind. His initial reaction had been for revenge. Now what should he do? His father was out there somewhere...that man who had killed his mother. Was revenge really sweet? Was revenge really justice? Dr. Collins had said he needed to let the police and courts take care of it. Was that enough to satiate his anger?

Dr. Collins checked into a Tucson motel close to the hospital so that he could spend several hours a day with Hunter. The seriousness of the tragedy Hunter was experiencing taxed Dr. Collins's counseling skills. But he did his best. His goal was to keep him talking about his anger in an effort to keep him from pushing it deep inside. As Hunter talked, Dr. Collins was able to validate the boy's feelings. After all, who wouldn't be angry and want revenge if faced with the same situation?

CHAPTER 29

Healing the Horse

HUNTER WAS RELEASED FROM the hospital a week later. He was given the choice of going home with his grandpa or returning to Promise Ranch. While there had never been a question in his mind, Smokey's visit on the fourth day cinched it. Sally was alive but struggling. Smokey was convinced that Hunter would be the answer to her recovery.

"She needs you. That little mare rescued you, now she needs you to rescue her," Smokey said. For a second, Hunter thought he saw tears in Smokey's eyes but the old cowboy turned away and when he turned back, his eyes were dry.

The drive back to the ranch in his grandpa's Suburban was long and uncomfortable. The pain pills that Hunter was given took the edge off but didn't exactly eliminate the pain anytime the road was bumpy.

"Hunter?" His grandpa broke the silence.

Hunter turned away from the window and looked as his grandfather.

"Hunter," William Mitchell said again, struggling to find the words, "you know you always have a home with your grandmother and me. We're a family. We need to stick together." His grandpa took his eyes off the road and looked over at Hunter, this only child of his beloved daughter.

Hunter nodded. "I appreciate that, Grandpa. But I can't leave Sally. She saved me. Now I need to see if I can save her."

Just then the car hit a bump, jostling Hunter. "Oh-h-h-h-h-h," Hunter groaned, gripping the arm rests.

"I'm sorry," his grandpa said. "I'll keep my eyes on the road."

The Suburban carrying Hunter and his grandpa drove under the Promise Ranch sign just before the sun went behind the clouds hanging over the western horizon. The bouncing of the car over the cattle guard created enough pain that Hunter struggled to keep conscious. Only his determination to see Sally kept him alert.

Hunter was so nervous to see his horse that his heart was pounding in his throat. Perspiration formed on his forehead even in the cooler than typical late December desert air.

"Can you take me to the barn?" he asked his grandpa hesitantly.

William Mitchell turned and drove past the cabins and down to the barn. Sally was not in her pen.

Hunter's grandpa got out of the car. "I'll be right back," he said before he shut the car door and walked into the barn. He came back a few minutes later with Smokey at his side.

Smokey's wrinkles were deeper than ever but his leathery face wore a broad smile as he walked up to Hunter's door. "Hunter! I'm so happy to see you. Thanks for coming back. As they say: 'You're just what the doctor ordered.'"

"How's she doing?"

"I don't want you to panic when you see her. She doesn't look very good. Her injuries are healing but it's her heart I'm worried about. She doesn't seem to have any desire to live. I'm hoping you can make a difference."

Hunter's grandpa came around with the wheelchair he had taken out of the back of the car. The old cowboy, still strong as an ox, lifted Hunter out of the car and settled him in the vinyl seat.

"Where is she?" Hunter asked looking up at Smokey.

"I have her all bedded down in a stall in the barn. She's not movin' around much."

As gently as he was able, he pushed Hunter across the barnyard and into the barn.

Hunter breathed in the smell of hay and leather as he tried to calm his beating heart. Smokey pushed him up to one of the stalls and opened the solid wood door. It took Hunter's eyes a minute to adjust to the darkness. When they did, he gasped.

Sally was lying on her side in a deep bed of fresh, yellow straw, the same position she had been in when he last saw her out on the desert floor. Without saying a word, he let his eyes examine her body. The deep puncture wounds on her neck and shoulder were covered with a thick salve. The expansive tear in her chest was sutured but would, undoubtedly, leave an ugly scar. Her eyes were closed and she was taking slow, shallow breaths. She was unaware that he was there...or, perhaps, she didn't care. Which was it?

"Sally," Hunter whispered. He waited for a response. One ear twitched slightly.

"Say it again," said Smokey.

"Sally," Hunter said, this time a little louder.

This time, Mustang Sally opened her eyes and looked right at the boy. Her ears pricked forward and she lifted her head a few inches off the straw. A soft nicker left her throat.

"Sally! Oh Sally!" choked out Hunter, desperately holding back the tears welling in his eyes.

Smokey clapped him on his shoulder. "See, I knew you were just what she needed!"

Hunter looked back at Smokey and his grandpa. "Can you take me to her?"

The two men lifted Hunter from the wheelchair and set him gently in the straw next to Sally's head. He bent over, lifted her pretty light brown head and placed it in his lap.

"I'm here and I won't ever leave you, Sally," he said as he stroked the long black forelock that fell down the length of her face. She closed her eyes and let out a long sigh. Hunter pressed his forehead against hers and let the tears pour though the gapping cracks in his heart.

The darkness gathered around them. Smokey brought out a blanket and pillow, well aware that there was no point in trying to talk Hunter into the house. A trip to the bathroom with the help of Smokey and William Mitchell, and a warm dinner provided by Betsy Fowler, and Hunter had all he needed to get him through the night.

For several hours, Hunter sat in the straw, rubbing Sally's neck. He listened to her breathing and the night sounds around him. He heard the rustling sound of mice scurrying around looking for spilled oats. A barn owl went in and out several times, silently hunting for those very same mice.

At some time during the night, Hunter's eyes closed and he slept. His dreams were peaceful and soothing. He was riding Sally across the desert toward an expansive pink sunset. They galloped until, together, they reached it and were enveloped by its warmth. All around them were more horses. One horse approached from the circle of the sun, carrying a rider of its own. As Hunter looked, he saw his mother holding out her hands to him from the back of the horse.

CHAPTER 30

Healing Together

HUNTER AWOKE WHEN SOMETHING as soft as velvet rubbed his cheek. Startled, he sat up and looked right into Sally's deep brown eyes, those eyes that always captured him and drew him to her. Sally was standing. The little mare was on all four feet, standing right in front of him.

Hunter struggled up into a sitting position, his left leg jutting out into the straw between Sally's front feet. He reached up with both hands and gently cradled her muzzle between them. "Sally, you're standing up! Are you feeling better, girl?"

Footsteps were heard outside the stall, and Smokey's face appeared over the top of the door. A big smile filled his face. His eyes twinkled. "You've done it, my boy. You've done it! I knew you could. I knew it all along."

Sometimes hearts can be quick to heal but body often takes much longer. Sometimes just the opposite is true. With Sally, the heart healed quickly and the body slowly followed. With Hunter, it seemed the broken leg would be strong long before his heart would be.

Over the next few days, Hunter progressed from the wheelchair to crutches. Under Hunter's watchful eye, Sally began eating and moving slowly around her stall. Trips to the bathroom or a quick shower were the only times he left her stall. Smokey did the house cleaning chores, removing manure and replacing it with clean straw. Mrs. Fowler brought the human meals, often staying in the stall to visit while the boy ate. She loved watching him devour his food, acting as though he would never get enough. Sally's appetite was just as large.

On the third day, Betsy Fowler brought Hunter's violin. "Music heals the soul. Maybe it will help heal your injuries as well," she said with a big smile as she gently set the case down on the straw next to Hunter.

Hunter looked up at Mrs. Fowler. "I've never played it in a barn before."

"I'll bet the acoustics will be fabulous," she said with a laugh.

Hunter reached over and unbuckled the clasps on the case. He carefully took out the bow and tightened the tension screw. Then he lifted the violin up to his shoulder and tested each string, making adjustments where needed. Lifting his right hand, he drew the bow across the strings. Sally pricked her ears and turned to face him. Hunter closed his eyes and began playing Vivaldi's *Winter*. Mrs. Fowler and Sally stood silently, awestruck by the beauty of the music. Hunter let himself get lost in what he was playing, letting his pain and emotions flow out of him with each note, with each stroke of the bow. When he finished, he opened his eyes and lowered the violin. He looked up at his audience. Betsy Fowler was smiling and tears flowed freely down her cheeks. Sally was standing in front of him, her head lowered, her eyes half closed as though in a dream state.

"That was beautiful," said Betsy Fowler in a whisper.

Hunter smiled. "Thank you. And thank you for bringing me my violin. Music does heal the soul."

A few days later, Smokey opened the stall door. "Time for you two to get some fresh air," said the old cowboy, his leathery face beaming.

"You think she's ready?" asked Hunter.

"I'm more worried about you than her!" he said with a jovial laugh.

Hunter struggled up onto one foot and grabbed his crutches. "You don't need to worry about me!" he responded, feeling that he needed to prove himself. "I can handle these crutches." Turning toward Sally he said, "Let's go, girl. Let's show this old cowboy how it's done."

"Who's old?" cried Smokey with mock incredulity.

With the set of his jaw reflecting his determination, and putting all his weight on his arms, Hunter swung his legs forward. Sally followed right behind.

Hunter quickly discovered that walking with crutches was much harder than he had ever expected, especially on the uneven ground of the barn and yard. Slowly and carefully he worked his way forward, too proud to admit that he was having trouble.

Shuffling horse and wobbly boy walked into the warm winter sunshine. Hunter stopped and let his eyes adjust to the brightness. Sally stopped right beside him and waited.

Hunter breathed in the desert smells of dried sage and deer grass. The sun bounced off his skin. The gentle breeze tousled his reddish blond hair. It was a little bit of heaven right there in Arizona. Getting impatient, Sally nudged his shoulder. She was ready to get moving.

"Okay, girl," Hunter chuckled. "Here we go!"

Hunter moved into the barnyard, judiciously placing his crutches on the uneven dirt surface then swinging his legs forward. It wasn't long before his arms and armpits began feeling the strain and he had to stop and rest.

Smokey was watching from the barn door, not concerned but empathetic. He had spent more than his share of time on crutches and he didn't envy Hunter the experience.

"You doin' okay, Pachelbel?" he called out.

Hunter looked back and nodded with a grin. Actually, he felt great. But then he turned to look at Sally. In the bright sunlight, the wound on her chest looked grisly, and he was shocked. The sight of it sickened him. He had to look away.

With head low, Sally limped along beside Hunter, careful not to knock his crutches. The going was slow but steady.

"Hey Pachelbel!"

Hunter looked up at the sound of Julius's cheerful greeting. A smile filled his face as he watched his cabin mate jog up to him.

"Hey, Julius! When did you get back?"

"Just now. But none too soon by the looks of you. Here I leave for a few weeks and look what happens to you. Obviously, you can't get along without me!" teased the handsome kid, flashing him a cocky smile.

"You're right about that," Hunter said, sincerely. He hadn't realized until just now how much he had missed Julius.

"Say, dude, I'm sure sorry about your mom. That really sucks."

Hunter's smile disappeared and his head dropped.

Julius reached out his hand and placed it gently on Hunter's shoulder. "I want you to know I'm here for you, man."

Hunter nodded his head. "I know." That was one thing he did know. He had learned that Julius was a loyal friend. It was one of the many qualities he admired about this tall, lanky kid. It was a quality that he wanted to develop...if he could ever quit feeling sorry for himself.

Julius stayed by his side as they made one loop around the yard. He helped him return to the barn and get Sally back in her stall. Julius was becoming quite a horseman in his own right and he immediately set about attending to the dun mare's needs. He brought her fresh water and feed. Then he grabbed the first aid kit and started cleaning and treating her many wounds, with special care given to the large wound on her chest.

When he was done, he looked over at Hunter who was leaning against the wall of the stall. "Hey man, I'm starving."

Hunter gave him half a smile. "Aren't you always?"

"Truer words were never spoken! Anyway, I would love some company for some of Mrs. Fowler's lunch."

A look of concern crossed Hunter's face as he turned to look at Sally. His hesitation was picked up immediately by Julius. "She'll be okay, Pachelbel. Look at her, she's just eating. We won't be gone long…just long enough to get something to eat ourselves. And a shower!"

Hunter looked up and smiled. "You trying to tell me something?"

"Well, I don't want to be rude but I've smelled pig sties that smell better than you!" Looking down at Hunter's cast he added, "How do you shower with that thing, anyway?"

CHAPTER 31

Holding On To Pain

OVER THE NEXT SEVERAL weeks, Hunter and Sally healed together. Their walks grew longer as they both became stronger. Sally was moved back to her pen, complete with new rails to replace the broken ones. Hunter moved back to the M Lazy C cabin.

His first day back in the cabin, he was given a tour of Julius's new aquarium including being introduced to each fish by name. Julius was absolutely beaming as he talked about his Christmas gift from Mr. Anderson. Hunter watched his face as he talked about each fish. Images of the day the two of them had found Julius's old aquarium broken to pieces on the floor and all of the fish lying dead on their sides flashed through his mind.

Yet Julius has been able to forgive Craig, he thought. *But a fish is not a mother,* he told himself. *A fish is just a stupid fish. Even if Julius did love them, there is really no comparison,* he argued, trying to justify his own unwillingness to forgive. In a way, he was right. Yet, forgiveness is always hard when something you love is taken away. He had struggled so hard to forgive his mother. Now that seemed like a walk in the park next to the impossible task of forgiving his father. That would never happen. *In fact,* he told himself, *it never should happen. The man is truly evil and he needs to pay for what he did.*

He was determined to make sure he did just that.

Hunter spent most of his time with Sally. If he wasn't with her, he was working on the computer, trying to keep up with his schoolwork. Each day, however, he searched the Internet for information on his father. He could find nothing helpful, and it appeared the police had made no progress whatsoever finding him. He seemed to have disappeared, even with the pictures that were sent out over the 'net and to every police department in the country.

At night, Hunter had nightmares about his father. Sometimes his mother was the victim. The details of his mother's death had been kept from him, but that didn't stop his imagination from creating one traumatizing scenario after another in his dreams.

Sometimes his father was coming after *him*. His father always appeared to be larger than life. His eyes were enormous and a cold, ice blue in color. His mouth was formed into a vicious sneer as he came toward him, closer and closer. Slowly the face started to melt, like wax exposed to heat, until it was quite unrecognizable. Only the eyes remained. Hunter would force himself to wake up to escape the terror that filled him.

Every time it happened, he opened his eyes to find Julius looking over at him, a look of sympathy on his face. "Another bad dream, huh?" his cabin mate said.

Hunter nodded, folded his arms under his head and stared at the ceiling. With his lips pursed together tightly, he tried to empty his brain of the images left behind by his dreams. He waited in the dark room for his heart to slow its pounding and his breathing to return to normal. He could tell that Julius was still awake, waiting for him if he needed to talk. Instead, he turned over on his side, as much as he was able with the cast, and closed his eyes.

Healing from a broken femur is not as difficult as healing a broken heart. Perhaps the broken heart was slowing everything down. It seemed Sally was doing much better and healing much faster. Each morning, she welcomed him with a whinny the moment he stepped around the last cabin. Smokey was taking care of her feeding and manure cleaning, claiming that Hunter's job was to heal her wounds. This the boy did by carefully cleaning and applying wound salve. By this time, only the large gash on her chest needed attention and even that was looking much better. It would surely leave an ugly scar but that couldn't detract from the renewed sparkle in her eye.

By the spring, Hunter was able to get out of his cast. His bone, due to the strength of youth and the titanium rod, healed perfectly and the doctor gave him the go ahead to get back in the saddle. He took it slowly at first. As anyone who has ridden a horse for the first time in a long time knows, your muscles are not going to cooperate. The second day, he could feel his legs complaining loudly. He smiled as Smokey and Julius teased him for walking like a "city slicker." He didn't care. He was just glad to be back in the saddle.

CHAPTER 32

Drill Team

DURING THE MONTHS THAT Hunter spent focused on helping Sally heal, he hardly noticed that several new boys had come to the ranch. Shorty was no longer the shortest, a fact that pleased the young boy greatly. A few months after Hunter was back in the saddle, Smokey had a job for him to do.

"I guess you noticed all the new boys that have come to the ranch," the old cowboy said one morning as the two of them fed the horses.

Hunter was a bit embarrassed to admit he hadn't paid any attention. "Uh...yeah, I guess."

Smokey's pale eyes twinkled with understanding. "No matter. They're here and I need you to help them."

"Me? How can I help them?"

"The little herd of mustangs that I adopted nine months ago - right when you arrived - are all doing well in their training. They need a job to do. We've got plenty of boys and plenty of horses with time on their hands. I want you to fill up that time."

Hunter was well aware that Smokey had "a bee in his bonnet" as Betsy Fowler would say. "Spit it out, Smokey," Hunter said with a chuckle.

"I want you to start the Promise Ranch Drill Team."

"The *what*?" Hunter said, screwing up his face in incomprehension.

"Ain't you never seen a mounted drill team before?"

Hunter shook his head.

"Well, the sheriff's posse used to have one. They're the coolest thing ya ever seen." Smokey led Hunter into the tack room that doubled as his office and flipped on the computer. A few clicks of the keyboard later and the two of them were watching a video clip of a mounted patrol riding patterns around an arena at a full gallop. Hunter was mesmerized. He had never seen anything like it. It looked like a blast to him!

That evening Hunter made an announcement right after dinner. "Listen up, everyone." The noise abated. "I have an exciting announcement to make. Smokey and I are going to start the first ever Promise Ranch Mounted Drill Team, and we have spots for the twelve best riders...well, eleven if you don't count me 'cause I'm doing it. Riding tryouts will be Saturday morning at 10 o'clock sharp."

For a moment, there was silence while the boys tried to figure out what a drill team was and if it was cool enough for them to want to participate in. They looked at their neighbors, trying to gauge how they should react. No one seemed to want to take the lead on that so they all just got up from the tables and left, all except Julius and Shorty.

Hunter stood there, rather bewildered at the lack of enthusiasm. Julius stepped up and slapped him on the back. "Well, I think that went rather well, don't you?"

Hunter looked at him and frowned. Julius responded with a wink of his eye.

"I'll do it! I don't know what a drill team is but if you're doin' it, I'm in!" the young boy said, the smile on his face and twinkle in his eye reflecting his excitement.

Hunter smiled. "Thanks, Shorty. I knew I could count on you."

The next day was not a pleasant one for Hunter. He had to endure constant cat calls.

"Hey man, look who's here! It's the drill sergeant."

"Yes Sir! Anything you say, Sir!"

"Can we scoop that horse poop for you, Sir?"

"Can we lick your boots?"

Betsy Fowler watched with sympathy from the kitchen door as the boys laughed and jeered. Hunter walked by, teeth and fists clenched, trying to ignore it. "Hunter, come in here. I have something for you," Betsy Fowler called out over the hoots and chortles.

Hunter, glad for the distraction, hustled into the kitchen.

"Sounds to me like you need a big piece of my cherry pie."

Hunter sat down at the little table. "Thanks. I'll take the pie and any advice you can give me."

"Looks like you're doin' just fine."

"Fine? I'm the laughing stock of the whole ranch just 'cause Smokey asked me to put together this stupid drill team!" Hunter answered, exasperation evident in his voice.

"Stupid?" Mrs. Fowler parroted.

"Well, maybe it's not stupid. In fact, it looks really cool. I think the boys would have a lot of fun. But nobody even wants to come."

"Let's just see what Saturday morning brings. You just might be surprised. Now, eat my pie or my feelings will be hurt."

After a sleepless Friday night, Hunter and Julius walked out to the barn to get the chores done.

"What if nobody comes?" Hunter grumbled under his breath.

"What do you mean? Shorty said he would come."

"We can't have a drill team with just three riders."

"Hey, maybe we could get Mrs. Fowler to ride."

Both boys busted up at the image of round Betsy Fowler galloping around the arena on a little mustang. Laughter does a body good and Hunter was grateful, once again, for Julius's outlook on life.

When he quit laughing, Hunter took a deep breath. "No, seriously. What will we do?"

"I say we get on our horses and have a lot of fun."

By the time 10 o'clock rolled around, Hunter and Julius had groomed and tacked up all twelve horses and had them tied to the fence in the arena. Smokey moseyed in from the back paddock where he had been fixing a gate and checked their work. Nodding his approval, he said, "I'm impressed, boys. You really are becoming horsemen."

Just then, Shorty and two other boys entered the arena from the far end. A few minutes later, two more boys entered, rather sheepishly. In the next five minutes, three more boys appeared. Julius elbowed Hunter in the ribs. "Oh ye of little faith," he whispered out of the side of his mouth while looking at the boys. Together they walked toward the approaching boys who were kicking up dust from the arena's soft dirt.

Hunter smiled and stopped, facing the boys. "Welcome, boys. Welcome to our first drill team practice." Hunter had planned just what he wanted to teach the boys during this first practice. What he hadn't planned on was that most of them didn't even know how to mount a horse, let alone ride. So, his plans were abandoned as he, Julius and Smokey started from the very beginning. "This is a saddle, this is the stirrup...now put your left foot in the stirrup, lift up and put your other leg over the horse...no, not like that, swing your leg over the *back* of the saddle."

And so it went for the two hours they had scheduled. By the end, all 10 riders were on a horse and walking around the arena. True, they were just walking nose to tail but at least they were on the back of the horse and moving.

Any boys who had come to hang over the fence and mock or belittle the riders were quickly sent on their way by Smokey. "At least they're brave enough to be out here trying. That's more than I can say for the likes of you."

"Yeah, like we'd *want* to do that. It looks so stupid," said the boy who was newest to the ranch, a tall, lanky seventeen year-old, well-practiced in talking back to adults. "Let's get outta here," he said, shoving his two cohorts.

Hunter watched them go and wondered why guys like him always had to have at least two boys around them at all times.

An extra lesson was added on Wednesday evenings and, after a while, the boys were actually trotting without falling off too many times. Overall, Hunter was pleased with how quickly the boys were learning. But even more importantly, not only were they learning to ride, they were actually enjoying it. In response to their pleas, Hunter added a Thursday evening practice as well.

After the first couple of practices, Hunter and Julius decided that grooming and tacking up every horse by themselves was a bad idea so they started teaching the team members how to do that. Each boy was assigned a horse for whom he was responsible. Julius spent a lot of time teaching the boys how to curry, brush and clean the hooves of the horse. A few boys learned the hard way how to set the hoof down without getting stepped on.

Hunter took them into the tack room and helped the boys find their horse's saddle and bridle. Draping the bridle over their shoulder, each boy lugged the heavy western saddle to their horse and held it while Hunter demonstrated how he slowly and gently saddled Sally. The little dun mare stood calmly while he placed the saddle pad and saddle on her back then tenderly tightened the cinch.

With three, and sometimes even four, long practices a week, the teens progressed quite quickly. They learned not only how to ride a horse and carry out the maneuvers Hunter was teaching them, but they learned how important teamwork was. If they didn't follow directions with exactness, they would end up running headlong into another horse and rider or find themselves embarrassed by being in the wrong place at the wrong time in a formation. They learned to follow their leader without argument for their own safety and that of the horse they had learned to not only respect but to love.

Hunter was developing the important qualities that a leader needs. He was learning how to communicate clearly. He was learning when to be lighthearted and when to be firm. He was learning how to encourage the discouraged and, perhaps most importantly, how to make each member of the team feel important.

Smokey and the other staff members spent many hours watching the transformation of this group of boys, a group that now consisted of the desired twelve and had a waiting list to boot. Smokey patted himself on the back as he saw how his plan was not only helping his horses but his young protégé, Hunter, as well. The wrinkles on his leathery face deepened as he smiled, clearly pleased with himself.

CHAPTER 33

The Performance

HUNTER NOTICED THAT THE morning air was cool and crisp, signaling the imminent arrival of fall. He glanced over toward the cottonwoods that lined the creek at the north end of the ranch and noticed how many leaves were now golden in color. He breathed in deeply, savoring the smell of the sage as he quickened his step to get to the barn and to Sally.

Smokey was waiting for him, a big smile stretching his brown face. "Come into my office, Pachelbel," he said, sweeping off his cowboy hat and bowing deeply.

Hunter snorted. "Okay, Smokey. What's this all about?"

"I have a surprise for you."

The old cowboy turned on the heel of his dusty, well-worn boot and tromped toward the tack room of the barn. Hunter followed closely behind. Smokey stopped at the door and pushed it open, motioning broadly for Hunter to enter. Hunter rolled his eyes at Smokey's dramatics and walked in. He stopped and his mouth dropped open. Hanging across the bridle hooks were beautiful matching red and white long-sleeved cowboy shirts. A quick count revealed twelve in number. Smokey stepped up to one of the shirts and flipped it around. Across the back was written "Promise Ranch Mounted Drill Team."

Hunter stood wide-eyed, mouth agape.

"Well, say something," said Smokey with a laugh.

"I...I...I don't know what to say. They're beautiful shirts. But what are they for?"

"Well the Drill Team, of course," answered Smokey.

"But why do we need matching shirts?"

"So you'll look good at our first performance."

"Performance?" said Hunter, raising his eyebrows.

"Yep," said Smokey, clearly enjoying the game he was playing. "The Promise Ranch Drill Team will be performing at the Arizona State Fair."

"What?"

"Yep," Smokey said with a nod of his head.

Hunter shook his head and stammered, "H-how did you do that?"

"I've been around a long time. I've got connections, ya know."

"When is it?"

"The beginning of October."

"October?" A stab of panic went through Hunter. "That's only four weeks away. Can we be ready?"

"You better be. I put my neck on the line for you boys."

Practices became more intense from that day forward. Music was added to the routine they were practicing and by the beginning of October, the boys felt as confident as could be expected considering none of them had ever performed before, other than in an elementary school play or a piano recital, or, in Hunter's case, a violin recital.

The attention the drill team members were receiving only served to increase the jealously felt by the boys who had chosen not to participate. The heckling increased but couldn't even scratch the surface of the shields the boys wore, an armor made of pride in a job well done and confidence that they could accomplish great things. Smokey, Betsy Fowler, and Dr. Collins watched silently and smiled.

The black road slithered beneath the large van like a snake. The spotty clouds projected animal-shaped shadows on the sand of the desert through which they drove. Twelve excited boys learned Smokey's country western songs, singing at the top of their lungs. Behind them, twelve nervous horses struggled to maintain their balance while the wind coming through the slats of the stock trailer whipped their manes into one another's faces. For the boys, the trip to the fairgrounds in Phoenix went quickly. To the horses, it was an endurance test.

They arrived at the Arizona State Fairgrounds late in the afternoon. The guard at the gate waved them through, and Smokey adroitly maneuvered the long stock trailer between and around the many other vehicles until they reached the barn where the horses were to be stabled. As soon as the van and trailer stopped, the boys jumped out, eager to check on their horses.

"Everyone take care of your own horse. Get 'em unloaded and walk them around while I check us in and find our stalls," directed Smokey.

With Smokey thus occupied, Hunter took the lead. One by one, the horses were unloaded from the stock trailer and handed to their team member. Hunter watched with pride as the boys claimed their horse, love in the eyes of both equine and human.

The horses looked fabulous. Before they left the ranch, each horse was bathed and groomed until their coats shone and their manes and tails glistened. Their legs were wrapped for the trip in red polo wraps and each horse sported a shiny new red halter and lead rope. They looked like a team already.

Once all of the horses were bedded down, water buckets and hay nets filled, the boys were released for an hour of fun at the arcade and carnival. "Be back in one hour," Smokey warned. "We have rehearsal at 7:30 p.m. sharp."

He really didn't need to remind the boys to be punctual. The importance of discipline was a lesson they had learned well enough through their many hours of practice. So, Smokey watched the boys disperse through the gathering crowds, confident they would return on time.

The boys blended right in with the people at the fair. Cowboy boots and hats were a welcome and familiar sight here. The boys played games, ate cotton candy, rode some of the carnival rides and flirted with the girls who were eager to catch their eye. But by the time the hour was up, all twelve boys were at their horses' stalls ready to tack up.

Anyone who has been in a theater production knows the curse of the dress rehearsal. This one was no different. It seemed that if anything could go wrong, it would and did. Despite all the efforts Smokey made back at the ranch to "de-spook" the horses, it was impossible to prepare them for everything that was going on at the fair. Flags and banners flapped in the desert breeze. A giant Ferris wheel turned in the background, its lights twinkling and changing colors. And perhaps scariest of all, every few minutes a roller coaster sent its cars with screaming occupants around its track and over its crests.

The smells were as odd as the sights from a horse's point of view. The smoke from the barbecue cookers wafted over the arena and mingled with the scent of burnt kettle corn and sweet cotton candy, strongly overpowering the smell of the horses' anxiety-produced sweat. When the music for the team's performance began playing over the loud speakers, not one horse was willing to enter the arena.

"Dismount, Hunter, and lead Sally in," Smokey advised.

Hunter did as he was told, got off Sally, took her reins and walked beside her into the arena. He walked her completely around the arena, their music playing overhead. After two laps around, he led her back out to where the rest of the team was struggling, trying to keep their horses calm. "Everyone, get off and follow me," he said to his teammates.

Each of the boys did as they were told.

"Let's walk once around the arena. Get into a single file line behind me." In a row, each mustang walked beside its trusted rider. The sights, sounds and smells of the fair seemed to press in on them from all sides. The mustangs clung to the side of their riders for comfort as they walked into the arena, breaking into a prance only occasionally, sweat soaking their coats.

After completing a loop around the arena, Smokey told them to reverse direction. "The horses need to see everything from both sides of their brains. Everything looks different to them from a different direction."

With the horses now in the arena, the boys mounted and walked their entire pattern. They were discovering the value of patience when working with a thousand pound animal, especially one with a strong flight instinct. By the end of the evening, they were performing their pattern at a full gallop, just as they had practiced at the ranch.

The boys had a great time over the next three days. They stayed at a motel just walking distance from the fairgrounds. They woke with the first hint of daylight to go to the barn to take care of their horses. Then they walked back to the motel for the free breakfast. While not as good as Betsy Fowler's, it was free and plentiful. They performed every afternoon and evening to the cheers of the crowds. As their reputation spread, the size of the audience increased, especially among teenage girls who decided cowboys were cute.

The boys were having the time of their lives.

CHAPTER 34

The Choice

BY FRIDAY NIGHT, HUNTER was getting tired. He took his responsibility as leader seriously and it weighed on him. He wasn't sure he liked the role of mother hen for eleven other boys and twelve horses. Julius and Shorty were easy to keep track of. Julius didn't need supervision and Shorty was always at his side. But the other boys needed quite a bit more chaperoning, especially those who particularly enjoyed the attention they were getting from the girls. Hunter had to admit he enjoyed that, too. But he was more concerned with everyone's welfare. He didn't want to disappoint Smokey and he certainly wasn't going to let anything come ahead of caring for the horses.

The Friday night performance was their best yet. The horses were getting comfortable in the new environment and were really beginning to show off. After the presentation, the boys dismounted, bedded down their mustangs and walked down the street to their motel. They were filled with excitement, much too energized to sleep. Smokey ordered pizzas and movies and the boys settled down in their rooms. One by one, sleep overcame them, except in the case of Hunter.

The boy lay in his bed, arms folded under his head. The neon light from the motel sign cast a red glow in the room, creating eerie shadows across the ceiling. The images that plagued his dreams several months ago were trying their best to return and he struggled to push them away. He wanted to shove them back in the corners of his brain where they had been hiding.

Hunter's thoughts went to Sally for comfort, and he decided he would go check on her. Quietly, so as not to disturb the other boys, he got dressed and tip-toed to the door.

"Where are you going?" It was Shorty.

Hunter stopped with his hand on the doorknob. He turned and whispered. "I can't sleep. I'm going to check on the horses to make sure they're okay."

"Hum-m-m," responded Shorty, dreamily, as he rolled over.

"Do you want some company?"

Hunter recognized Julius's voice. "Naw. I'm fine. Go back to sleep." He slipped out the door into the cool desert night.

The few blocks that he had to walk took him by a late-night bar. Rock music and raucous laughter worked their way out the front door as Hunter hurried by. When he reached the barn, he was glad for the familiar and soothing sounds of the horses munching on their hay, occasionally snorting, and quietly moving around their stalls. He opened Sally's stall door and silently slipped inside. The dim light from the few ceiling lights that had been left on reflected in Sally's eyes as she turned to look at him. She let out a soft nicker in greeting. Hunter was sure she welcomed his company.

"Hi girl," Hunter whispered as he stepped up to her head. He reached out his hand and rubbed her forehead beneath the thick, black forelock. She lifted her muzzle to his cheek and blew out warm air from her nostrils. Hunter reached in his pocket and pulled out a sugar cube, which he offered to her. While she savored the sweet taste of the treat, he ran his hands along her light brown neck and across her back. Her coat was soft and healthy, a result of the wonderful care she received at his hands. Even in the dimness of the stall, it seemed to glow. The boney hips and ribs that once pressed against the skin were now covered with a smooth layer of fat and well-developed muscles. Hunter was pleased with the results of the care he had provided her over that last year.

It was well after midnight when Hunter bid Sally farewell, did one final check-up on each of the other horses, and left the barn. The fairgrounds were deserted. The Ferris wheel loomed dark and still over the carnival grounds. Paper cups and wrappers littered the pavement, reminders of the many people who had been there earlier. A run-away balloon drifted by, its string dangling down. Hunter paused and looked around. The fairgrounds looked much different after everyone had gone home for the night.

Hunter exited the fairgrounds through the participant's gate, waving at the guard who sat, half asleep, in the station. He walked down the street toward the motel whose red, neon sign blinked on and off, beckoning all to come inside. He was finally feeling ready to sleep and he looked forward to putting his head on the pillow. He smiled as he walked along, thinking about Sally and the bond they had between them. Hunter really didn't know how other people felt about their horses, but he couldn't imagine that anyone loved their horse more than he did. They had been through too much together. After all, they had saved each other's lives. No, in his mind, their bond was unique. And perhaps it was.

Hunter was lost in his happy thoughts of Sally as he approached the bar. Suddenly, the doors to the bar flung open and a man stumbled out, helped by the bartender. "Go home and sleep it off," the proprietor said as he shoved the man directly toward Hunter.

The man twisted and turned, pivoting wildly on one leg then the other before collapsing on the sidewalk at Hunter's feet. Startled, Hunter jumped back. Unsure what he should do, he looked from side to side to see if there was anyone who could help him. Seeing no one, he stepped up to the man who was lying face down on the hard concrete.

The boy reached down and gently rolled the man over. Hunter gasped and jumped back. His heart seemed to stop beating. His body turned rigid, just a step away from rigor mortis. Everything felt terribly wrong. First the surroundings began to go, the brick buildings, the chipped concrete sidewalks, the sound of traffic on the street, the loud music and voices from within the bar. Next, the man's booted feet and denim-covered legs seemed to disappear. Soon all that remained was his face. This face Hunter had seen only once before but this face he would never forget.

Images.

Brutal images.

Images consumed him and filled his heart with dread.

Lying on the concrete, prone and helpless at his feet, was his father. The stiffness dissolved and Hunter's body began to shake uncontrollably. He felt as though he needed to vomit.

He had to be sure. Perhaps his mind was playing tricks on him. He began searching the man's pockets. That's when he found it. Tucked into the front jacket pocket, Hunter's fingers touched the grip of a handgun. Slowly, his fingers wrapped around it and he paused. Sweat beaded up on his forehead and ran down between his shoulder blades as an internal debate played out in his mind.

Slowly, he pulled the gun from the pocket and stood, his feet planted a foot apart, his back slightly arched. He looked down at the man. Yes. He was sure. This man...this man lying passed out at his feet, was indeed his father.

His mind began racing, playing out the different options now placed before him. Here was his chance to get the revenge he wanted. The desire for revenge had never left him. Buried perhaps, but only buried in a shallow grave. Easily retrieved. This man deserved to die. He had lived a wasted life. He had abandoned them. He had killed his mother. His *mother*. The person he loved most in life.

Resolve filled his entire being, and he slowly raised the hand that held the gun. Hunter moved his other hand up and grasped the gun with both hands to steady his shaking. He closed his eyes and slowed his pulse. He didn't want to blow his one chance.

Hunter released the safety and placed his right index finger on the trigger. The damaged boy opened his eyes, let out a long breath then clenched his jaw, feeling the veins on his forehead pulse. He spread his feet and stretched forth his arms, pointing the gun at the man's chest.

"Hunter! What are you doing?"

Through the mist of darkness that filled his soul, Hunter recognized Julius's voice. Without turning around he answered through clenched teeth. "Go away, Julius. Let me take care of this on my own."

Julius had awakened to discover Hunter's empty bed. Sensing that something was wrong, he dressed quickly and left the motel. He never expected to see his best friend standing over a man, pointing a gun at his chest. Now he needed to figure something out...and fast.

"Hunter, talk to me. What's going on here?"

"I said GO AWAY!" Hunter hissed, still staring at the target of his hatred.

"I'm not going anywhere without you. So tell me what you're doing," Julius responded, his quiet voice concealing the panic he felt within.

"This is my *father*," Hunter said, spitting out the last word as though it left a bad taste in his mouth.

Understanding washed over Julius and his panic turned into a cold-white fear. He pressed his lips tightly together and pressed his fists against his head. He knew he had to handle this correctly.

"You can't do this, Hunter. Let me have the gun. This is a huge mistake."

For just a moment, Hunter looked away from the man on the sidewalk and glared at Julius. "You say I can't do this? That it's a mistake? Even mistakes can have a good feeling about them," he yelled.

Julius was shocked at the look in Hunter's eyes. He had never seen his friend look like this. The thought flashed through his mind that he was in over his head. This appeared to be one battle he would lose. Then a thought entered his mind.

"Are you going to let him win?"

"What do you mean by that?" Hunter said, turning back to stare down at his intended victim. "Looks like *I'm* the winner. He has been delivered into my hands and I intend to take full advantage of it."

"You kill him and he wins."

"I don't see how."

"Think! What happens next? You do this and you'll spend the rest of your life in jail."

"So? He's still dead. He can't hurt anyone else if he's dead."

"Like I said: he wins."

"How can you say *he* wins?"

"If you do this, the rest of *your* life will be destroyed. He will win by destroying you."

Hunter didn't respond. He was out of responses.

Julius sensed a chink in Hunter's armor. He saw a glimmer of hope. "Give me the gun, Hunter. I'll guard him and you can have the pleasure of calling the police. You can be the one to send him to prison for the rest of *his* life."

Julius held his breath and waited. At that moment, Julius felt someone step up beside him. He turned and looked. Relief filled him as he looked into Smokey's leathery face.

Smokey seemed to know immediately what was happening. "Hand me the gun, son."

Something about Smokey's calm but authoritarian manner pierced Hunter's weakened armor. Without looking away from his father, he dropped one hand and extended the other with the gun toward Smokey. The old cowboy grabbed the gun.

Julius stepped forward and embraced his friend. "You won, Hunter. You won," he whispered.

Their tears mingled.

Epilogue

THE WHINNIES FILLED THE air, amplified by the metal roof of the trailer. Hooves stomped and kicked at the sides and floorboards. The entire trailer shook on its tires as it waited to be relieved of its cargo.

The cowboy stepped up to the rear door and unlatched the gate. Keeping the door between himself and the tons of horse flesh it contained, he pulled opened the door. The eight mares, and four young soon-to-be-gelded stallions pushed their way around and charged out the opening. A dun-colored mare with striking black legs and a glossy black mane and tail was waiting to greet them. The little mare tossed her head and whinnied. She ran around the new horses as though catching them in a lasso of her own making. Soon, she had them corralled at the far end of the arena.

The cowboy shut the trailer door and climbed through the rails of the fence. He walked up to an old man who was sitting and dozing in the shade provided by the barn.

"Hey, Smokey, come see the horses I picked out from the BLM auction."

The old cowboy lifted his head and pushed back his cowboy hat. His face was lined like a board that had been left out in the sun for too long. But his pale eyes twinkled with enthusiasm and he smiled warmly. He extended his hands and the younger man pulled him out of the chair. Slowly, Smokey shuffled to the side of the arena, supported by his helper.

The younger man let out a long, low whistle. "Sally, bring 'em 'round here." Immediately, the little mare named Sally whinnied and reared up on her hind legs. Lowering herself to the ground, she shook her head and pranced toward the little herd, pushing them forward.

The twelve new mustangs broke into a run and circled the arena. The old cowboy watched each one carefully, his experienced eyes looking for qualities that only he could see. He turned to look at his young companion. "Ya done well, Pachelbel. Mighty fine horses ya picked out. 'Course they're a little skinny but that's to be expected. Other than that, they look like they're in good health and sound as a dollar. Yep...ya done well." He gave his protégé a pat on the shoulder with one hand as he steadied himself against the fence with the other.

"Thanks, Smokey," said Hunter, truly pleased that he had passed the test. Never before had he been entrusted to do the purchasing for the ranch without Smokey. But Smokey had become too frail, content now to just sit in the shade and let the sun rise and set without his help.

Hunter looked around and noticed a young boy peering through the rails.

"Hey, you must be the new boy. I'm Pachelbel and this is Smokey. I'm in charge of the horses here at Promise Ranch. Do you like horses?"

"Nah. If they don't have wheels and a motor, I don't ride 'em," said the boy with a sneer.

Smokey elbowed Hunter and chuckled softly under his breath. Hunter smiled back then turned to the boy and said, "Well, there's a lot of horses here that need training and I sure could use some help."

Acknowledgements

AS A HORSE-LOVER since birth, I have always believed in "training" a horse, not "breaking" a horse. Training a horse takes kindness and patience and a lot of knowledge. There are several great trainers around the country who teach clinics to help people work lovingly with horses. The methodology that Smokey uses in this book is taken from the two Clinton Anderson clinics I attended. I sat on the edge of my chair each day as I was researching for this book and took careful notes. If you are interested in training a horse, I suggest you study with one of the several excellent horse trainers who teach clinics.

I also want to express my gratitude to Dr. Elia Gourgouris, an outstanding counselor in Boulder, Colorado, who works with youth and families. He is also the co-author of the fabulous book, *7 Paths to Lasting Happiness*. He generously gave of his time to read and comment on the chapters I wrote that depicted Dr. Collins working with Hunter.

My appreciation also goes out to the many organizations around the west that work tirelessly to protect the wild mustang herds. If you need a great charity to contribute to, I would suggest one of these. You can search the Internet for "Wild Mustang Charities" and find several that would love your contribution.

Special Note to Youth and Adult Book Clubs

Discussion questions about this book are

available on the website:

www.dancinghorsepress.com

About the Author

Award-winning author, M.J. Evans, grew up in Lake Oswego, Oregon. Upon graduation from Oregon State University and marriage to her high school sweetheart, she spent five years teaching at the High School and Junior High levels. She retired from teaching to raise the couple's five children.

Ms. Evans is an avid equestrian. She loves competing in Dressage and trail riding in the beautiful Colorado Mountains.

Connect with her on her website: **mjevansbooks.com** or **dancinghorsepress.com**

Additional titles by this Author

The Mist Trilogy:
Mom's Choice Award Gold Medal Winner
Behind the Mist
Mists of Darkness
The Rising Mist

North Mystic
First Place winner of the Purple Dragonfly
Award and Finalist in the Colorado Author's
League Awards

Equestrian Trail Guide Books:
Riding Colorado-
Day Trips from Denver with Your Horse
Riding Colorado II-
Day Trips from Denver with Your Horse
Riding Colorado III-
Day AND Overnight Trips with Your Horse

Coming next:
The Centaur Chronicles

"Like" these books on Facebook:

Behind the Mist
North Mystic
In the Heart of a Mustang

Learn about the noble and great horses
throughout history. Follow the author's blog:
www.themisttrilogy.blogspot.com

23839346R00226

Made in the USA
Lexington, KY
17 December 2018